By Lawrence Block

The Burglar in the Closet

The Burglar in the Closet

Lawrence Block

Random House : New York

for Mary Pat, who opened the right door

Myst
Biock
Bu

Copyright © 1978 by Lawrence Block

All rights reserved under International and Pan-American Copyright
Conventions. Published in the United States by Random House, Inc., New
York, and simultaneously in Canada by Random House of Canada Limited,
Toronto.

Library of Congress Cataloging in Publication Data
Block, Lawrence.
The burglar in the closet.
Sequel to Burglars Can't Be Choosers.
I. Title.
PZ4.B6523BU   [PS3552.L63]   813'.5'4 78–57116
ISBN 0–394–42374–7

Manufactured in the United States of America
9 8 7 6 5 4 3 2
First Edition

Sir, he who would earn his bread
writing books must have the assurance
of a duke, the wit of a courtier, and
the guts of a burglar.

—*Dr. Samuel Johnson*

The Burglar in the Closet

One

"Gramercy Park," said Miss Henrietta Tyler, "is an oasis in the middle of a cruel sea, a respite from the slings and arrows of which the Bard has warned us." A sigh escaped her lips, the sort of sigh that follows upon the contemplation of an oasis in the middle of a sea. "Young man," she said, "I do not know what I would do without this blessed green plot. I simply do not *know* what I would *do.*"

The blessed green plot is a private park tucked into Manhattan's East Twenties. There is a fence around the park, a black wrought-iron fence seven or eight feet high. A locked gate denies access to persons who have no legal right to enter. Only those persons who live in certain buildings surrounding the park and who pay an annual fee toward its maintenance are issued keys that will unlock the iron gate.

Miss Henrietta Tyler, who was seated on the green bench beside me, had such a key. She had told me her name, along with much of her personal history, in the fifteen minutes or so we'd been sitting together. Given time, I was fairly sure she'd tell me everything that had occurred in New York since her birth, which I calculated had taken place just a year or two after Napoleon's defeat at Waterloo. She was a dear old thing, was Miss Henrietta, and she wore a sweet little hat with a veil. My grandmother used

3

to wear sweet little hats with veils. You don't see them much anymore.

"Absence of dogs," Miss Henrietta was saying. "I'm ever so glad they don't allow dogs in this park. It's the only spot left in the city where one may walk without constantly scanning the pavement beneath one's feet. A disgusting animal, the dog. It leaves its dirt anywhere at all. The cat is infinitely more fastidious, isn't it? Not that I would care to have one underfoot. I've never understood this compulsion people have to bring animals into their houses. Why, I wouldn't even care to have a fur coat. Let that sort of thing stay in the forest where it belongs."

I'm sure Miss Henrietta wouldn't have talked thus to a stranger. But strangers, like dogs, are not to be found in Gramercy Park. My presence in the park indicated that I was decent and respectable, that I had a rewarding occupation or an independent income, that I was one of Us and not one of Them. My clothes had certainly been chosen to reinforce that image. My suit was a tropical worsted, a windowpane check in light and dark gray. My shirt was light blue with a medium-length button-down collar. My tie carried stripes of silver and sky blue on a navy field. The attaché case at my feet was a slim model in cocoa Ultrasuede that had cost someone a pretty penny.

I looked, all in all, like a bachelor taking a breather in the park after a hard day in a stuffy office. Perhaps I'd stopped somewhere for a bracing brace of martinis. Now I was taking some air on this balmy September evening before I trotted on home to my well-appointed apartment, there to pop a TV dinner in the microwave oven and inhale a beer or two while the Mets dropped a squeaker on the tube.

Well, not quite, Miss Henrietta.

No hard day, no stuffy office. No martinis, because I do not permit myself so much as a sniff of the cork when I am about to go to work. And there's no microwave oven in my modest apartment, and no TV dinners either, and I stopped watching the Mets when they traded Seaver. My apartment's on the Upper West Side, several miles from Gramercy Park, and I didn't pay a cent for the Ultrasuede attaché case, having appropriated it some months ago while liberating an absent gentleman's coin collection. I'm sure it had cost *him* a pretty penny, and God knows it contained any number of pretty pennies when I waltzed out the door with it in hand.

Why, I didn't even have a key to the park. I'd let myself in with a cunning little piece of high-tempered German steel. The lock on the gate is a shockingly simple one to pick. It's surprising more people don't let themselves in when they want to spend an hour away from dogs and strangers.

"This business of running around the park," Miss Henrietta was saying. "There goes one of them now. Look at him, won't you?"

I looked. The chap in question was around my age, somewhere in his middle thirties, but he'd lost a good deal of his hair. Perhaps he'd run out from under it. He was running now, or jogging, or whatever.

"You see them day and night, winter and summer. There's no end to it. On cold days they wear those suits, sweating suits I believe they're called. Unbecoming gray things. On a warm night like tonight they wear cotton shorts. Is it healthy to carry on like that, do you suppose?"

"Why else would anyone do it?"

Miss Henrietta nodded. "But I can't *believe* it's good for one," she said. "It looks so *unpleasant.* You don't do anything of the sort, do you?"

"Every once in a while I think it might be good for me. But I just take two aspirin and lie down until the thought passes."

"I believe that's wise. It appears ridiculous, for one thing, and nothing that looks so ridiculous can possibly be good for you." Once more a sigh escaped her lips. "At least they're constrained to do it *outside* the park," she said, "and not *inside* the park. We've that to be thankful for."

"Like the dogs."

She looked at me, and her eyes glinted behind the veil. "Why, yes," she said. "*Quite* like the dogs."

By seven-thirty Miss Henrietta was dozing lightly and the jogger had run away somewhere. More to the point, a woman with shoulder-length ash-blond hair and wearing a paisley print blouse and wheat-colored jeans had descended the stone steps in front of 17 Gramercy Park West, glanced at her watch, and headed around the corner on Twenty-first Street. Fifteen minutes had passed and she had not returned. Unless the building had held two women of that description, she was Crystal Sheldrake, the future ex-wife of Craig Sheldrake, the World's Greatest Dentist. And if she was out of her apartment it was time for me to go into it.

I let myself out of the park. (You don't need a key to do that, or even a piece of high-tempered German steel.) I crossed the street, attaché case in hand, and mounted the steps of Number Seventeen. It was four stories tall, an exemplary specimen of Greek Revival architecture thrown up early in the nineteenth century. Originally, I suppose, one family had sprawled over all four floors and stowed their luggage and old newspapers in the basement. But standards have crumbled, as I'm sure Miss Henrietta could have told me, and now each floor was a separate apartment. I studied the four bells in the vestibule, passed up the ones marked Yalman, Porlock, and Leffingwell (which, taken as a trio, sounds rather like a firm of architects specializing in industrial parks) and poked the one marked Sheldrake. Nothing happened. I rang again, and nothing happened again, and I let myself in.

With a key. "The bitch changed the lock," Craig had told me, "but she couldn't hardly change the one downstairs without getting the neighbors steamed at her." Having the key saved me a couple of minutes, the lock being a rather decent one. I pocketed the key and walked to the elevator. It was in service though, the cage descending toward me, and I decided I didn't much want to meet Yalman or Porlock—Leffingwell lived on the first floor, but I decided it might even be he in the elevator, returning to base after watering his rooftop garden. No matter; I walked on down the hallway to the stairs and climbed two flights of carpeted steps to Crystal Sheldrake's apartment. I rang her bell and listened to two-tone chimes within, then knocked a couple of times, all in the name of insurance. Then I put my ear to the door and listened for a moment, and then I retrieved my ear and went to work.

Crystal Sheldrake's door had not one but two new locks, both of them Rabsons. The Rabson's a good lock to begin with, and one of these was equipped with their new pickproof cylinder. It's not as pickproof as they'd like you to think but it's not a plate of chopped liver either, and the damn thing took me a while to get past. It would have taken even longer except that I have a pair of locks just like it at home. One's in my living room, where I can practice picking it with my eyes closed while I listen to records. The other's on my own door, keeping out burglars less industrious than I.

I picked my way in, albeit with my eyes open, and before I even locked the door behind me I took a quick tour of the apartment. Once upon a time I didn't bother to do this, and it later turned out that there was a dead person in the apartment, and the situation proved an embarrassment of the rankest order. Experience is as effective a teacher as she is because one does tend to remember her lessons.

No dead bodies. No live bodies except my own. I went back and locked both locks, plopped my attaché case upon a Victorian rosewood love seat, slipped my hands into a pair of skintight sheer rubber gloves, and went to work.

The name of the game I was playing was Treasure Hunt. "I'd like to see you strip the place to the four walls," Craig had said, and I was going to do my best to oblige him. There seemed to be more than four walls—the living room I'd entered, a full dining room, a large bedroom, a small bedroom that had been set up as a sort of den and television parlor, and a kitchen with a fake brick floor and real brick walls and a lot of copper pots and pans hanging from iron hooks. The kitchen was my favorite room. The bedroom was all chintzy and virginal, the den angular and uninspired, and the living room an eclectic triumph featuring examples of bad taste down through the centuries. So I started in the kitchen and found six hundred dollars in the butter compartment of the refrigerator door.

Now the refrigerator's always a good place to look. A surprising number of people keep money in the kitchen, and many of them tuck it into the fridge. Cold cash, I suppose. But I didn't pick up the six hundred by playing the averages. I had inside information.

"The slut keeps money in the refrigerator," Craig had told me. "Usually has a couple hundred stashed in the butter keeper. Keeps the bread with the butter."

"Clever."

"Isn't it just? She used to keep marijuana in the tea canister. If she lived where people have lawns she'd probably store it with the grass seed."

I didn't look in the tea canister so I don't know what kind of tea it contained. I put the cash in my wallet and returned to the living room to have a shot at the desk. There was more money in the top right-hand drawer, maybe two hundred dollars at most in fives and tens and twenties. It wasn't enough to get excited about but I was getting excited anyway, the automatic tickle of excitement that starts working the instant I let myself into someone else's abode, the excitement that builds every time I lay hands on someone else's property and make it my own. I know this is all morally reprehensible and there are days when it bothers me, but there's no getting around it. My name is Bernie Rhodenbarr and I'm a thief and I love to steal. I just plain love it.

The money went in my pocket and became my money, and I started skimming through the other drawers in the little kneehole desk, and several in a row contained nothing noteworthy and then I opened another and right on top were three cases of the sort that good watches come in. The first one was empty. The second and third were not. One of them was an Omega and the other was a Patek Philippe and they were both gorgeous. I closed the cases and placed them in my attaché case where they belonged.

The watches were choice but that was it for the living room and it was actually more than I'd expected. Because the living room like the kitchen was just a warm-up. Crystal Sheldrake lived alone, although she often had overnight guests, and she was a woman with a lot of valuable jewelry, and women keep their jewelry in the bedroom. I'm sure they think they do it so it's handy when they're getting dressed, but I think the real reason is that they sleep better surrounded by gold and diamonds. It makes them feel secure.

"It used to drive me crazy," Craig had said. "Sometimes she left things lying out in plain sight. Or she'd just toss a bracelet and a necklace in the top drawer of the bedside table. She had the bedside table on the left-hand side, but I suppose they're both hers now so check 'em both." No kidding. "I useta beg her to keep some of that stuff in a safe-deposit box. She said it's too much trouble. She wouldn't listen to me."

"Let's hope she didn't start listening recently."

"Not Crystal. She never listened to anybody."

I took my attaché case into the bedroom with me and had a

look for myself. Earrings, finger rings, bracelets, necklaces. Brooches, pendants, watches. Modern jewelry and antique jewelry. Fair stuff, good stuff, and a couple things that looked, to my reasonably professional eye, to be very good indeed. Dentists take in a certain amount of cash along with the checks, and hard as it may be to believe this, some of that cash doesn't get reported to the Internal Revenue people. Some of it gets turned quietly into jewelry, and that jewelry could now get turned just as quietly right back into cash again. It wouldn't bring in what it had cost in the first place, since your average fence is a rather more careful customer than your average dentist, but it would still amount to a fairly impressive sum when you consider that it all started out with nothing but a whole lot of toothaches and root-canal work.

I searched very carefully, not wanting to miss anything. Crystal Sheldrake kept a very neat apartment on the surface, but the interiors of her drawers were a scandal, with baubles and beads forced to keep company with rumpled panty hose and half-full make-up jars. So I took my time, and my attaché case grew heavier as my fingers grew lighter. There was plenty of time. She had left the house at seven-fifteen and would probably not return until after midnight, if indeed she returned before dawn. Her standard operating procedure, according to Craig, called for a drink or two at each of several neighborhood watering holes, a bite of dinner somewhere along the way, and then a few hours devoted to a combination of serious drinking and even more serious cruising. Of course there were nights that got planned in advance, dinner engagements and theater dates, but she'd left the house dressed for a casual night's entertainment.

That meant she'd either bring home a stranger or go to a stranger's home, and either way I'd be long gone before she recrossed her own threshold. If they settled on his place, the jewels might be fenced before she knew they were missing. If she brought the guy home and they were both too sloshed to notice anything was missing, and if he in turn let himself out before she woke up, she might just tag the crime on him. Either way I looked to be in the clear, and enough thousands of dollars ahead so that I could coast for the next eight or ten months, even after I gave Craig his share. Of course it was hard to tell just what the attaché case contained, and it's a long, long way from jewelry to cash, but things were looking good for Mrs. Rhodenbarr's boy Bernard, no question about it.

I remember having that thought. I can't begin to tell you what a comfort it was a little later when Crystal Sheldrake locked me in the bedroom closet.

Two

The problem, of course, derived from an offshoot of Parkinson's Law. A person, be he bureaucrat or burglar, tends to take for a task as much time as is available for it. Because I knew Crystal Sheldrake would be absent from her apartment for hours on end, I was inclined to spend several of those hours divesting her of her possessions. I've always known that burglars should observe the old *Playboy* Philosophy—i.e., Get In and Get Out—but there's something to be said for making use of the available time. You can miss things if your work is rushed. You can leave incriminating evidence behind. And it's a kick, going through another person's things, participating vicariously (and perhaps neurotically) in that person's life. The kicks involved are one of the attractions of burglary for me. I can admit that, even if I can't do anything much about it.

So I lingered. I could have tossed the Sheldrake *pied-à-terre* in twenty efficient minutes if I put my mind to it. Instead I took my precious time.

I'd finished picking the second Sheldrake lock at 7:57—I happened to note the time before easing the door open. At 9:14 I closed my attaché case and fastened the snaps. I picked it up and noted its increased weight with approval, trying to think of the avoirdupois more in terms of carats than ounces.

Then I set the case down again and gave the premises another careful contemplative toss. I don't even know if I was really looking for anything at this point. A person younger than I might have said I was trying to pick up vibrations. Come to think of it, I might have said that myself, but not aloud. What I was probably trying to do, in truth, was prolong the delicious feeling of being where I wasn't supposed to be and where no one knew I was. Not even Craig knew I was there. I'd told him I would go in a night or two later, but it was such a pleasant evening, such a propitious night for breaking and entering . . .

So I was in the bedroom, examining a pastel portrait of a youngish woman elegantly coiffed and gowned, with an emerald at her throat that looked to be head and shoulders above anything I'd stolen from Crystal Sheldrake. The painting looked early nineteenth century and the woman looked French, but she might simply have cultivated the art of looking French. There was something fetching about her expression. I decided she'd been disappointed so many times in life, largely by men, that she'd reached a point where she expected disappointment and decided that she could live with it, but it still rather rankled. I was between women myself at the time and told her with my eyes that I could make her life a joy and a fulfillment, but her chalky blues met mine and she let me know that she was sure I'd be just as big a letdown as everybody else. I figured she was probably right.

Then I heard the key in the lock.

It was a good thing there were two locks, and it was another good thing I'd relocked them upon entering. (I could have bolted them as well, so that they couldn't be opened from outside, but I'd given up doing that a while ago, figuring that it just let citizens know there was a burglar inside and moved them to come back with a cop or two in tow.) I froze, and my heart ascended to within an inch or two of my tonsils, and my body got damp in all those spots the antiperspirant ads warn you about. The key turned in the lock, and the bolt drew back, and someone said something inaudible, to another person or to the empty air, and another key found its way into another lock, and I stopped being frozen and started moving.

There was a window in the bedroom, conventionally enough, but there was an air conditioner in it so there was no quick way to open it. There was another smaller window, large enough so that I could have gotten through it, but some spoilsport had installed bars on it to prevent some rotten burglar from climbing in through it. This also prevented rotten burglars from climbing out, although the installer had probably not had that specifically in mind.

I registered this, then looked at the bed with its lacy spread and thought about throwing myself under it. But there wasn't really a hell of a lot of room between the box spring and the carpet. I could have fit but I could not have been happy about it. And there's something so undignified about hiding under a bed. It's such a dreary cliché.

The bedroom closet was every bit as trite but rather more comfortable. Even as the key was turning in the second Rabson lock, I was darting into the closet. I'd opened it before to paw through garments and check hatboxes in the hope that they held more than hats. It had then been quaintly locked, the key stuck right there in the lock waiting for me to turn it. I don't know why people do this but they do it all the time. I guess if they keep the key somewhere else it's too much trouble hunting for it every time they want to change their shoes, and I guess locking a door provides some sort of emotional security even when you leave the key in the lock. I'd taken nothing from her closet earlier; if she had furs they were in storage, and I hate stealing furs anyway, and I certainly wasn't going to make off with her Capezios.

At any rate, I hadn't bothered relocking the closet, and that saved unlocking it all over again. I popped inside and drew it shut after me, slipped between a couple of faintly perfumed gowns and adjusted them again in front of me, took a deep breath that didn't even begin to fill my aching lungs, and listened carefully as the door opened and two people entered.

It was not hard to know that there were two of them because I could hear them talking, even though I could not yet make out their conversation. From the pitch of their voices I could tell that one was female and one was male, and I assumed the female was Crystal Sheldrake, wheat jeans and paisley blouse and all. I had no idea who the man might be. All I knew was that he was a fast worker, having hustled her back here so swiftly. Maybe he was married. That would explain his hurry, and why they'd wound up here rather than at his place.

Sounds of ice clinking, sounds of liquid pouring. I breathed in the closet smells of Arpège and Shalimar and antique perspiration and thought wistfully of the two before-dinner martinis I'd neglected to have. I never drink before I work because it might impair my efficiency, and I thought about that policy, and I thought about my efficiency, and I felt rather stupider than usual.

I hadn't had the before-dinner drinks and I hadn't had the dinner either, preferring to postpone that pleasure until I could do it in style and in celebration. I'd been thinking in terms of a latish supper at a little hideaway I know on Cornelia Street in the Village. Those two marts first, of course, and then that cold asparagus soup they do such a good job with, and then the sweetbreads with mushrooms, God, those sweetbreads, and a salad of arugola and spinach with mandarin orange sections, ah yes, and perhaps a half bottle of something nice to go with the sweetbreads. A white wine, of course, but what white wine? It was something to ponder.

Then coffee, lots of coffee, all of it black. And of course a postprandial brandy with the coffee. No dessert, no point in overdoing it, got to watch the old waistline even if one's not quite obsessive enough to jog around Gramercy Park. No dessert, then, but perhaps a second snifter of that brandy just to take the edge off all that coffee and reward oneself for a job well done.

A job well done indeed.

In the living room, ice continued to clink in glasses. I heard laughter. The radio or the record player was pressed into service. More ice clinking. More laughter, a little more carefree now.

I stood there in the closet and found my thoughts turning inexorably in the direction of alcohol. I thought about the martinis, cold as the Klondike, three hearty ounces of crystal-clear Tanqueray gin with just the most fleeting kiss of Noilly Prat vermouth, a ribbon of twisted lemon peel afloat, the stemmed glass perfectly frosted. Then my mind moved to the wine. Just what white wine would be ideal?

"... beautiful, beautiful evening," the woman sang out. "Know something, though? I'm a little warmish, sweetie."

Warmish? I couldn't imagine why. There were two air conditioners in the apartment, one in the bedroom and one in the living room, and she'd left them both running in her absence. They'd kept the apartment more than comfortable. My hands are always warm and sweaty inside my rubber gloves, but the rest of me had been cool and dry.

Until now, that is. The bedroom air conditioner was having no discernible effect on the air on the closet, which was not what you'd call conditioned. My hands were getting the worst of it and I peeled my gloves off and stuck them in my pocket. At the moment fingerprints were my least pressing concern. Suffocation probably headed the list, or at least it seemed to, and close behind it came apprehension and arrest and prison, following one upon the other in a most unpleasent way.

I breathed in. I breathed out. Maybe, I thought, just maybe, I could get away with this one. Maybe Crystal and her gentleman friend would be sufficiently involved in one another so as not to notice the absence of jewelry. Maybe they'd do whatever they'd come to do, and having done it perhaps they'd leave, or lapse into coma, and then maybe I could let myself out of the closet and the apartment. Then, swag in hand, I could return to my own neighborhood and—

Hell!

Swag in hand indeed. My swag, all of it neatly packed in the Ultrasuede attaché case, was not by any means in hand, not in hand and not at hand either. It was resting on the opposite side of the bedroom from me, propped against the wall under the pastel portrait of the disappointed mademoiselle. So even if Crystal didn't notice the absence of her jewelry she seemed more than likely to notice the presence of the case, and that would indicate not merely that she had been burgled but that the burglar had been interrupted while at work, and that would mean she would put in an urgent phone call to 911, and cop cars would descend upon the scene of the crime, and some minion of the law would be bright enough to open the closet, and I, Bernard Grimes Rhodenbarr, would be instantly up the creek, and in no time at all, up the river as well. Hell!

"Something more comfortable," the woman said. I could hear them better now because they were en route to the bedroom, which I can't say astonished me. And then they were in the bedroom, and then they did what they'd come to the bedroom to do, and that's all you're going to hear from me on that subject. It was no fun listening to it and I'm certainly not going to try to re-create the experience for you.

As a matter of fact, I paid them the absolute minimum of attention myself. I let my mind return to the question of the perfect wine as accompaniment to the sweetbreads. Not a French white, I decided, for all that the sweetbreads were a French dish. A German white might have a little more oomph. A Rhine? That would do, certainly, but I decided after some thought that a choice Moselle might carry a wee bit more authority. I thought about a Piesporter Goldtröpfchen I'd had not long ago, a bottle shared with a young woman with whom, as it turned out, that was all that was to be shared. That would be acceptable with the sweetbreads, certainly. One wouldn't want anything too dry. And yet the dish did call for a wine with a slight lingering sweetness, a fruity nose—

Of course! My mind summoned up memories of a '75 Ockfener Bockstein Kabinett, with a full, lovely flowery scent, a tart freshness of flavor like a bite out of a perfect Granny Smith apple, the merest hint of spice, just a trace of tongue-tickling spritz. There was no guarantee that the restaurant I'd chosen would have that particular wine, but neither was there any guarantee that I'd be having dinner there instead of doing five-to-fifteen at Attica, so I might as well give my imagination free rein. And what was that nonsense about a half bottle of wine? Any wine worth drinking was worth having a full bottle of, surely.

I rounded out my meal somewhat by guessing what the vegetable *du jour* might chance to be. Broccoli, I decided, steamed *al dente,* uncomplicated with Hollandaise—just dotted lightly with sweet butter. Or, failing that, some undercooked zucchini sauced very lightly with tomato and basil and dusted with grated Parmesan.

My thoughts then jumped sensibly enough to the after-dinner brandy. A good Cognac, I thought. Any good Cognac. And I let myself dwell on various good Cognacs I'd had at one time or another and the ever-more-comfortable circumstances than the present in which I'd relished them.

A drink, I thought, would help. It might not *really* help, but it would seem to help and I'd settle for that just now. A well-equipped burglar, I told myself, really ought to be supplied with a hip flask. Or even a square flask. A thermos, perhaps, to keep the martinis properly chilled . . .

Nothing lasts forever. The lovemaking of Crystal Sheldrake and her latest friend, which certainly seemed eternal to me if not to them, lasted by actual measurement twenty-three minutes. I can't say when Crystal's key turned in her lock, having had more urgent matters on my mind at the time. But I did glance at my watch not too long after and noted that it was 9:38. I glanced again when the two of them entered the bedroom. 10:02. I checked again from time to time while the performance was in progress, and when the finale descended with a crash my glow-in-the-dark watch told me it was 10:25.

There was a spate of silence, a chorus of *Gee, you were terrific* and *You're sensational* and *We've got to do this more often,* all the things good up-to-date people say instead of *I love you.* Then the man said, "Christ, it's later than I thought. Half-past ten already. I better get going."

"Running back home to what's-her-name?"

"As if you didn't remember her name."

"I prefer to forget it. There are moments, my sweet, when I actually manage to forget her existence altogether."

"You sound jealous."

"Of course I'm jealous, baby. Does that come as a surprise to you?"

"Oh, come on, Crystal, you aren't really jealous."

"No?"

"Not a chance."

"Think it's just a role I play? Maybe you're right. I couldn't say. Your tie's crooked."

"Mmm, thanks."

They went on like this, not saying anything I had any enormous need to hear. I had trouble keeping all of my mind on their conversation, not only because it was duller than a Swedish film but because I kept waiting for one or the other of them to stub a toe on the attaché case and wonder aloud how it happened to be there. This, however, did not happen. There was more chitchat, and then she walked him to the door and let him out and locked up after him, and I think I heard the sound of her snicking the sliding bolt shut. Fine precaution to take, lady, I thought, with the burglar already tucked away in your clothes closet.

Then I heard nothing at all for a while, and then the phone rang twice and was answered, and there was a conversation which I couldn't make out. More silence, this time followed by a temper tantrum of brief duration. "Stinking sonofabitch bastard," Crystal roared, out of the blue. I had no way of knowing whether she was referring to her recent bedmate, her ex-husband, her telephone caller, or someone else altogether. Nor did I too much care. She yelled out just once, and then there was a thudding sound, perhaps of her heaving something at a wall. Then calm returned.

And so did Crystal, retracing her steps from living room to bedroom. I guess she had replenished her drink somewhere along the way, because I heard ice cubes clinking. By now, however, I no longer actively wanted something wet. I just wanted to go home.

The next thing I heard was water running. There was a lavatory in the hallway off the living room, a full bathroom off the bedroom. The bathroom had a stall shower and that's what I was hearing. Crystal was going to erase the patina of love-making. The man had left and Crystal was going to take a shower and all I had to do was pop out of the closet and scoop up my jewel-laden attaché case and be gone.

I was just about to do this when the shower became suddenly more audible than it had been. I shrank back behind the rack of dresses and sundry garments, and footsteps approached me, and a key turned, neatly locking me in the closet.

Which of course was not her intent. She wanted to unlock the door, and she had left it locked and assumed it was still locked, so she'd turned the key, and—

"Funny," she said aloud. And paused, and then turned the key in the opposite direction, this time unlocking the closet, and reached in to take a hooded lime-green terry-cloth robe from a hanger.

I did not breathe while this was happening. Not specifically to escape detection but because breathing is impossible when your heart is lodged in your windpipe.

There was Crystal, ash-blond hair stuffed into a coral shower cap. I saw her but she didn't see me, and that was just fine, and in the wink of an eye (if anyone's eye winked) she was closing the door again.

And locking it.

Wonderful. She had a thing about closets. Some people can't leave a room for five minutes without turning off the lights. Crystal couldn't walk away from an unlocked closet. I listened as her footsteps carried her back to the bathroom, listened as the bathroom door closed, listened as she settled herself under her pulsating massagic shower head (no speculation; I'd looked in the bathroom and she had one of those jobbies).

Then I stopped listening and poked between the dresses and turned the doorknob and pushed, and when the door predictably refused to budge I could have wept.

What an incredible comedy of errors. What a massive farce.

I stroked the lock with my fingertips. It was laughable, of course. A good kick would have sent the door flying open, but that would involve more noise than I cared to create. So I'd have to find a gentler way out, and the first step was to get the damned key out of the lock.

Which is easy enough. I supplied myself with a scrap of paper by tearing one of the protective garment bags that was protecting one of Crystal's garments. I scrunched down on hands and knees and slipped the paper under the door so that it was positioned beneath the keyhole. Then I used one of my little pieces of steel to poke around in the silly-ass lock until the key jiggled loose and fell to the floor.

Back on my hands and knees again, tugging at the paper. Tugging gently, because a swift tug would have the effect of a swift yank on a tablecloth, removing the cloth but leaving the dishes behind. I didn't just want the paper. I wanted the key that was on it as well. Why pick a lock if the key's just inches from your grasp? Easy does it, take your time, easy, that's right—

And then the door buzzer buzzed.

I swear I wanted to spit. The damned buzzer made a sound loud enough to make hens stop laying. I froze where I was, praying fervently that Crystal wouldn't hear it under the shower, but evidently my prayer wasn't quite fervent enough. Because the thing sounded again, a long horrible piercing blurt, and while it was so doing Crystal shut off the water.

I stayed where I was and I went on tugging at the scrap of paper. The last thing I wanted was for her to spot the key on the floor on her way to the door. The key cleared the door and came into view, and while this was happening the bathroom door opened and I heard her footsteps.

I stayed where I was, crouched on the floor as if in prayer. If she noticed that the key was missing, well, at least she wouldn't be able to open it because I had the key. That, I told myself, was something.

But she didn't even slow down as she passed the closet. She swept right on by, presumably in her lime-green terry-cloth robe. I suppose she poked the answering buzzer to unlatch the downstairs door. I waited, and I suppose she waited, and then the doorbell sounded its two-tone chime. Then she opened the door.

By this time I had gotten to my feet again and was standing behind the rack of dresses. I was also paying close attention to what was happening, but it was hard for me to get a clear picture of what was going on. The door opened. I heard Crystal saying something. Part of what she said was inaudible, but I could make out *"What is it? What do you want?"* and similar expressions. It seems to me that there was panic in her voice, or at the least a whole lot of apprehension, but I may have just filled that in after the fact.

Then she said *"No, no!"* very loud, and there was no missing the terror. And then she screamed, but it was a very brief scream, chopped off abruptly as if it were a recording and someone lifted the tone arm from the record.

Then a thudding sound.

Then nothing at all.

And there I was, standing snugly in my closet like the world's most cautious homosexual. After a moment or two I thought about using the key in my hand to unlock the door, but then once again I heard movement outside. Footsteps, but they sounded different from Crystal's. I couldn't say that they were lighter or heavier. Just a different step. I'd grown used to Crystal's footsteps, having spent so much time lately listening to them.

The footsteps approached, reached the bedroom. The source of the footsteps began moving around the bedroom, opening drawers, moving furniture around. At one point the doorknob turned but of course the door was still locked. Whoever had turned the knob was evidently not proficient at picking locks. The closet was abandoned and I was safe inside it.

More movement. Then, after what couldn't really have been an eternity, the footsteps passed me again and returned to the living room. The apartment's outer door opened and closed—I'd learned to recognize that sound.

I looked at my watch. It was eleven minutes to eleven, and thinking of it that way made it more memorable than 10:49. I looked at the key I was holding and I slipped it into the lock and turned it, and then I hesitated before opening the door. Because I had all too good an idea what I'd find there and it wasn't anything I was in a rush to look at.

On the other hand, I was really sick of that closet.

I let myself out. And found, in the living room, pretty much what I'd expected. Crystal Sheldrake, sprawled out on her back, one leg bent at the knee, the foot cramped beneath the opposite thigh. Blond hair in shower cap. Green robe open so that most of her rather spectacular body was exposed.

An ugly purple welt high on her right cheekbone. A thin red line, sort of a scratch, reaching from just below her left eye to the left side of her chin.

More to the point, a gleaming steel instrument plunged between her noteworthy breasts and into her heart.

I tried to take her pulse. I don't know why I made the attempt because God knows she looked deader than the Charleston, but people are always taking pulses on television and it seemed like the thing to do. I spent a long time taking hers because I wasn't sure I was doing it right, but finally I gave up and said the hell with it.

I didn't get sick or anything. My knees felt weak for a moment, but then the sensation lifted and I was all right. I felt rotten because death is a rotten thing and murder is particularly horrible, and I felt vaguely that there should have been something I could have done to prevent this particular murder, but I was damned if I could see what it was.

First things first. She was dead and I couldn't help her, and I was a burglar who certainly did not want to be found at the scene of a far more serious crime than burglary. I had to wipe off whatever surfaces might hold my fingerprints and I had to retrieve my attaché case and then I had to get the hell out of there.

I didn't have to wipe Crystal's wrist. Skin doesn't take fingerprints, any number of inane television programs notwithstanding. What I did have to wipe were the surfaces I'd been near since I took off my rubber gloves (which I now put back on, incidentally). So I got a washcloth from the bathroom and I wiped the inside of the closet door and the floor of the closet, and I couldn't think what else I might have touched but I wiped around the outside closet knob just to make sure.

Of course the murderer had touched that knob. So maybe I was wiping away *his* prints. On the other hand, maybe he'd been wearing gloves.

Not my concern.

I finished wiping, and I went back to the bathroom and put the washcloth back on its hook, and then I returned to the bedroom for a quick look at the disappointed pastel lady, and I gave her a quick wink and dropped my eyes to look for my attaché case.

To no avail.

Whoever killed Crystal Sheldrake had taken her jewelry home with him.

Three

It never fails. I open my mouth and I wind up in hot water. But in this case the circumstances were special. After all, I was only following orders.

"Open, Bern. A little wider, huh? That's right. That's fine. Perfect. Just beautiful."

Beautiful? Well, they tell me it's in the eye of the beholder and I guess they're right. If Craig Sheldrake wanted to believe there was beauty in a gaping mouthful of teeth, that was his privilege and more power to him. They weren't the worst teeth in the world, I don't suppose. Twenty-some years ago a grinning orthodontist had wired them with braces, enabling me to shoot those little rubber bands at my classmates, so at least they were straight. And since I'd given up smoking and switched to one of those whiter-than-white toothpastes, I looked somewhat less like a supporting player in *The Curse of the Yellow Fangs.* But all of the molars and bicuspids sported fillings, and one of the wisdom teeth was but a memory, and I'd had a wee bit of root-canal work on the upper left canine. They were respectable teeth for one as long in the tooth as I, perhaps, and they'd given me relatively little trouble over the years, but it would be an exaggeration to call them either a thing of beauty or a joy forever.

A stainless-steel probe touched a nerve. I twitched a little and

23

made the sort of sound of which one is capable when one's mouth is full of fingers. The probe, relentless, touched the nerve again.

"You feel that?"

"Urg."

"Little cavity, Bern. Nothing serious but we'll tend to it right now. That's the importance of coming in for a cleaning three or four times a year. You come in, we shoot a quick set of X-rays just as a routine measure, we have a look around, poke the old molars a bit, and we catch those little cavities before they can grow up into big cavities. Am I right or am I right, keed?"

"Urg."

"All this panic about X-rays. Well, if you're pregnant I suppose it's a different story, but you're not pregnant, are you, Bernie?" He laughed at this. I've no idea why. When you're a dentist you have to laugh at your own jokes, which might be a hardship but I suspect it's more than balanced by the fact that you remain blissfully unaware of it when your precious wit goes over like a brass blimp. Since the patient can't laugh anyway, his silence needn't be interpreted as a reprimand.

"Well, we'll just take care of it right away before I turn you over to Jillian for a cleaning. First molar, lower right jaw, that's a cinch, we can block the pain with Novocaine without numbing half your head in the process. Of course some practitioners of the gentle art would wind up depriving you of sensation in half your tongue for six or eight hours, but you're in luck, Bern. You're in the hands of the World's Greatest Dentist and you have nothing to worry about." Chuckle. "Except paying the bill, that is." Full-fledged laugh.

"Urg."

"Open a little wider? Perfect. Beautiful." His fingers, tasting as though they'd been boiled, deftly packed my mouth with cylinders of cotton. Then he took a curved piece of plastic tubing attached to a long rubber tube and propped it at the root of my tongue, where it commenced to make slurping noises.

"This is Mr. Thirsty," he explained. "That's what I tell the kids. Mr. Thirsty, come to suck up all your spit so it doesn't gum up the works. Of course I don't put it quite so crudely for the little tykes."

"Urg."

24

"Anyway, I tell the kids this here is Mr. Thirsty, and when I whack 'em out with nitrous oxide I tell 'em they're going for a ride in Dr. Sheldrake's Rocket Ship. That's 'cause it gets 'em so spacy."

"Urg."

"Now we'll just dry off that gum there," he said, peeling back my lower lip and blotting the gum with a wad of cotton. "And now we'll give you a dab of benzocaine, that's a local that'll keep you from feeling the needle when we jab a quart of Novocaine into your unsuspecting tissue." Chortle. "Just kiddin', Bernie. No, you don't have to give a patient a liter of the stuff if you have the skill to slip the old needle into the right spot. Oh, thank your lucky stars you've got the World's Greatest Dentist on your team."

The World's Greatest Dentist shot me painlessly with Novocaine, readied his high-speed drill, and began doing his part in the endless fight against tooth decay. None of this hurt. What was painful, albeit not physically, was the patter of conversation he directed my way.

Not at first, though. At first everything was fine.

"I'll tell you something, Bernie. You're a lucky man to have me for a dentist. But that's nothing compared to how lucky *I* am. You know why? *I'm* lucky to *be* a dentist."

"Urg."

"Not just because I make a decent living. Hell, I don't have any guilt on that score. I work hard for my money and my charges are fair. I give value for value received. The thing about dentistry is it's very rewarding in other ways. You know, most of the dentists I know started off wanting to be doctors. I don't know that they had any big longing for medicine. I think half the time the attraction was that their parents thought it was a great life. Money, prestige, and the idea that you're helping humanity. Anybody'd be happy to help humanity with all that money and prestige there as an added incentive, right?"

"Urg."

"Speak up, Bern, I can't hear you." Chuckle. "Just joking, of course. How we doing? You in any pain?"

"Urg."

"Of course you're not. The WGD strikes again. Well, all these guys went to dental school instead. Maybe they couldn't get accepted at medical school. A lot of bright guys can't. Or maybe they looked at all that education and training stretching out in front of them, four years of med school and two years internship and then a residency, and when you're a kid a few years looks like a lifetime. Your perspective on time changes when you get to be our age, but by then it's too late, right?"

I guess we were about the same age, getting a little closer to forty than thirty but not quite close enough to panic about it. He was a big guy, taller than me, maybe six-two or six-three. His hair was a medium brown with red highlights, and he wore it fairly short in a deliberately tousled fashion. He had an open honest face, long and narrow, marked by warm brown eyes and a long down-curving nose and sprinkled with freckles. A year or two back he'd grown a mustache of the macho variety sported by male models in men's cologne ads. It was redder than his hair and didn't look quite bad enough for me to counsel him to shave it off, but I sort of wished he would. Beneath the mustache was a full mouth overflowing with the nicest teeth you could possibly imagine.

"Anyway, here you've got a load of dentists who secretly wish they were doctors. Some of them don't even keep it a secret. And you've got others who went into dentistry because, hell, a man has to go into something unless he wants to go on welfare, and it looked like a decent deal, set your own hours, a steady buck, no boss over you, some prestige, and all the rest of it. I was one of this group, Bern, but in my case something wonderful happened. Know what it was?"

"Urg?"

"I fell in love with my work. Yep, that's what happened. One thing I recognized right off the bat is dentistry's about solving problems. Now they're not problems of life and death, and I'll tell you, that's fine with me. I sure as hell don't want patients dying on me. The doctors are welcome to all that drama. I'd rather deal with smaller life questions, like Can This Tooth Be Saved? But a man comes in here, or a woman, and I look around and take X-Rays, and there's a problem and we deal with it then and there."

No *urg* this time. He was rattling along too well to need encouragement from me.

"I'm just so damn lucky I wound up in this line of work, Bern. I remember my best friend and I were trying to decide what we wanted to do with our lives. I picked dental school and he went into pharmacy school. His educational route looked easier and his potential income was certainly much higher. You own your own store, you branch out and open other stores, hell, you're a businessman, you can make a ton. For a little while there I wondered if maybe I shouldn't have taken the road he took. But just for a little while. Jesus, can you picture me standing behind a counter selling Kotex and laxatives? I couldn't be a businessman, Bern. I'd be rotten at it. Hey, open a little wider, huh? Perfect, beautiful. I'd be rotten at it and I'd go out of my bird with boredom. I read somewhere that pharmacists get more action than any other occupational group. Some study out of California. I wonder if it's true or not? What woman would want to ball a druggist, anyway?"

He went on with this line of thought and my mind drifted off a ways. I was a captive audience if there ever was one, and I had to sit there and take it but I didn't, by God, have to pay attention.

And then he was saying, "So I sure as hell wouldn't want to be a pharmacist, and I swear I wouldn't want to be anything but what I am. Satisfied Sam, huh? True, though."

"Urg."

"But I'm normal, Bernie. I have fantasies just like everybody else in this world. I try to think what I'd be if dentistry just didn't happen to be an option for me. Just asking myself the hypothetical question, like. And because it's hypothetical and I *know* it's hypothetical, why, I can feel free to indulge myself. I can pick something that would call for someone a lot more adventurous than I actually know myself to be."

"Urg."

"I try to have fantasies of being a professional athlete, for instance. I play a lot of squash and a fair amount of tennis, and I'm not absolutely lousy, in fact I'm getting so I shape up pretty decent on the squash court, but there's such an obvious gulf between my game and the pro game that I can't even fantasize about playing that role. That's the trouble with reality. It gets in the way of the best fantasies."

"Urg."

"So I've settled on something I'd like to be, and I can enjoy it on a fantasy level because I know virtually nothing about it."

"Urg?"

"It's exciting, it's adventurous, it's dangerous, and I can't say I don't have the skills or temperament for it because I don't know exactly what they are. I gather it pays a whole lot and the hours are short and flexible. And you work alone."

"Urg?" He had me interested by now. It sounded like the sort of thing I might be interested in.

"I was thinking about crime," he went on. "But nothing where you have to point guns at people or where you wind up with them pointed at you. In fact I'd want a criminal career with no human contact involved in it at all. Something where you work alone and don't have to be a part of a gang." Chuckle. "I've pretty much narrowed it down, Bernie. If I had it to do all over again, and if dentistry was just out of the picture, I'd be a burglar."

Silence.

"Like you, Bernie."

More silence. Lots of it.

Well, of course it rocked me. I'd been set up with considerable skill. Here was ol' Craig Sheldrake, Mr. Laid Back and World's Greatest Dentist, just running pleasantly off at the mouth about how much he loved his work, and the next thing I knew he'd dropped this brick into my open mouth and all the Novocaine in the world couldn't have numbed the shock.

You see, I've always kept my personal and professional lives as separate as possible. Except during my blessedly infrequent stays as a guest of the state, at which times one's freedom of association is severely proscribed, I don't hang out with known criminals. My friends may swipe stationery from the office or buy a hot color TV. They almost certainly fiddle a bit on their income tax returns. But they don't make their livings lifting baubles from other people's apartments, or knocking over liquor stores and filling stations, or writing checks drawn on the Left Bank of the Wabash. Their moral caliber may be no greater than mine but their respectability quotient is infinitely higher.

And as far as any of them know, I'm as respectable as the next fellow. I don't talk much about my work, and in the sort of casual friendships toward which I gravitate there's nothing remarkable about that. It's generally understood that I'm in investments, or living on a small but apparently adequate private income, or doing

28

something dull but earnest in import-export, or whatever. Sometimes I'll assume a more colorful role to impress a youngish person of the interesting sex, but for the most part I'm just Good Old Bernie, who always has a buck in his pocket but never throws it around recklessly, and you can always count on him for a fifth at poker or a fourth at bridge, and he probably does something like sell insurance but hasn't thank God tried to sell it to *me*.

Now my dentist evidently knew I was a burglar. The fact that my cover was blown wasn't horrible—there were people in my apartment building who knew, and a few other folks around town. But the whole thing was startling, and so was the manner in which it had all been brought to my attention.

"Couldn't resist that," Craig Sheldrake was saying. "Damn if you didn't just about drop your lower incisors on my linoleum. Didn't mean to shake you up but I couldn't help myself. Hell, Bern, it don't make no never mind to me. You had your name in the paper when they were trying to hang a murder charge on you a year or so ago and I happened to notice it. Rhodenbarr's not the most common name in the world, and they even gave your address, which I of course have in the files, so it looked to be you all right. You've been in a few times since then and I never said anything because there was never any need."

"Urg."

"Right—but there is now. Bernie, how'd you like to rack up a really nice score? I guess different burglars like to steal different things but I never heard of a one who doesn't like to steal jewelry. I'm not talking about crap from the costume counter at J. C. Penney. I'm talking about the real stuff. Diamonds and emeralds and rubies and lots of fourteen- and eighteen-carat golderoo. Stuff any burglar would be proud to stash in his swag bag."

I wanted to tell him not to use what he evidently thought was thieves' argot. But what I said was "Urg."

"You betcha, Bern. But open a little wider, huh? That's the ticket. Let me get to the point. You remember Crystal, don't you? She worked for me, but that was before your time. Then I made the mistake of marrying her and lost a great dental hygienist who put out and gained in return a slovenly wife who also put out— for half the world. But I know I've told you my troubles with that bitch. I poured that tale into any ear that would stand still for it."

How could any ear escape it when it shared a head with a mouth with Mr. Thirsty slurping up the saliva?

"Bought her all the jewelry in the world," he went on. "Sold myself on the idea that it was a good investment. I couldn't just hold onto money, Bern. Not built that way. And she gave me this song and dance about investing in jewelry, and I had all this undeclared cash I couldn't invest in stocks and bonds, it had to go into something where you can pay cash and keep the whole thing off the books. And you can get good bargains in the jewelry line if you'll do business that way, believe me."

"Urg."

"Thing is, then we went and got divorced. And she got all the pretties, and I couldn't even pitch a bitch in court or the IRS might stand up and start wondering where the cash for those pretties came from in the first place. And I'm not hurting, Bern. I make a good living. But here's this bitch sitting on a couple hundred thousand dollars in jewelry, plus she got the house and everything in it, the co-op apartment on Gramercy Park with a key to the fucking park and everything, and I got my clothes and my dental equipment, and on top of that I pay her a healthy chunk of alimony every month, which I have to pay until she dies or remarries, whichever comes first, and personally I wish that what comes first is her death and that it comes yesterday. But she's healthy, and she's smart enough not to remarry, and unless she drinks and screws herself to death I'm on the hook forever."

I'm not divorced, never having gotten married in the first place, but it seems to me that everyone I know is either divorced or separated or thinking of moving out. Sometimes, when they all carp about alimony and child-support payments, I feel vaguely out of it. But most of the time what I feel is grateful.

"You could knock her off easy," he went on, and then he began explaining just how I could go about it and when she was apt to be off the premises and all the rest. He went into greater detail than you have to know about, with me supplying the *urgs* whenever he stopped for air or zeroed in for some serious work on the old molar. When the drilling was done he had me rinse and then he set about putting in a filling, and throughout the whole process I heard just what an easy score it would be and how profitable I would find it, and more than anything else, what a bitch she was and how she had it coming. I suppose a lot of this last part was rationalization. Evidently he figured I would be happier stealing from a bad person than a good one. In point of fact I've found that it doesn't make much difference to me, and that what I really prefer is to burgle a victim about whom I know absolutely nothing. This business works best when you keep it as impersonal as you can.

He went on, did Craig Sheldrake, World's Greatest Dentist, and so did the elaborate process of filling my tooth. And finally his conversation was finished and so was my tooth, and Mr. Thirsty made his exit and so did all the now-sodden wads of cotton, and there was a spate of rinsing and spitting, and bit of opening wide a final time while the great man checked the results of his handiwork, and then I sat back in the chair while he stood beside me, I examining my remodeled tooth with the inquisitive tip of my tongue, he holding one hand with another and waiting to ask the urgent question.

"Well, Bern? Have we got a deal?"

"No," I said. "Absolutely not. Out of the question."

I wasn't just fencing. I damn well meant it.

See, I like to find my own jobs. There are a lot of burglars who love to work on the basis of inside information, and God knows there's a lot of such information to be had. Fences are a prime source of this sort of data. A fence will oftentimes contact a thief, not merely with a request for a particular item but with the specs and location of the item all written out for him. This is an easy way to work and a lot of burglars are crazy about it.

And the jails are full of them.

Because what do you really know when you're dealing with a fence? Receivers of stolen goods are a curious breed, and there's something unquestionably slimy about the greatest portion of them. If I had a daughter, I certainly wouldn't want her to marry one. A fence does something manifestly illegal but he rarely does a single hour behind bars for his sins, partly because it's hard to nail him with the evidence, partly because his crime is the sort there's little public outcry against, and partly because he's apt to be pretty clever at playing both sides against the middle. He may pay off cops, and if paying them off with cash and furs doesn't work, he may turn to paying them off by setting up other criminals for them. I don't say that you're likely to get set up if you take jobs a fence hands you, but I've managed to dope out one thing in my time. If you're the only one who knows you're going to pull a particular job, then nobody's in a position to rat on you. Any trouble you fall into is either your own damn fault or the luck of the draw.

Now I certainly wasn't worried about Craig setting me up. There was little chance of that. But he liked to talk, accustomed as he was to all those immobile ears, and who could say when it would seem like a good idea to talk about the clever job he and good old Bernie Rhodenbarr had pulled on sluttish Crystal?

Ahem.

Then how did I wind up in the very same Crystal's apartment while someone was stopping her heart?

Good question.

Greed, I guess. And perhaps a portion of pride. Those were two of the seven deadly sins and between them they'd done me in. The Gramercy Park apartment sounded as though it would yield a sizable score with minimal risk and no special security equipment to overcome. There are no end of apartments every bit as easy to get into but most of them contain nothing more valuable or portable than a color TV. Crystal Sheldrake's place was a prime grade-A target, the only drawback being that Craig would know about my role in the deal. With the state of my bankroll what it was, which is to say slim indeed, this objection gradually paled to the point of invisibility.

Pride came into it in a curious way. Craig had gone to great lengths to talk about what a groovy thing it was to be a burglar, how it was adventurous and all, and while that may have been largely a build-up to that *Like you, Bernie* punch line, it still was not without effect. Because, damn it all, I guess I see what I do as glamorous and adventurous and all the rest of it. That's one reason I find it impossible to stop making surreptitious visits to other people's residences, that plus the fact that the only job for which I have any training is making license plates, and you have to be behind bars to pursue that career.

A thought occurred to me, although not until later. I may have known all along I was going to go for the deal. I may have acted reluctant in order to keep the World's Greatest Dentist from expecting too much in the way of a finder's fee. I don't think I was aware of that aim, but aware or not it worked pretty well. I don't know what Craig may have had in mind to ask, but in the course of talking me into changing my mind his percentage dropped to a fifth of whatever I netted when the take was fenced. Now that was eminently fair, considering that Craig got to sit home in front of the television set, never fearful of being shot or arrested in the name of justice. But he was an amateur, and amateurs rarely have a sense of proportion about these matters, and he could easily have wanted as much as half if I'd been eager from the start.

No matter. When he got down to twenty percent I suppressed an urge to see just how far down he'd go—he obviously wanted her to lose the jewels more than he wanted his own share of the proceeds. And I caved in and told him I'd do the dirty deed.

"Fantastic," he said. "Super. You'll never regret it, Bern."

Even then, I wished he hadn't said that.

I stayed in the dental chair. Craig went off, doubtless to boil his hands before facing another patient, and in no time at all Jillian took over. I was encouraged to lean back in my chair again while she picked and poked at my teeth and gums, liberating tartar, scaling, and doing all the unpleasant chores that come under the heading of dental cleaning.

Jillian didn't talk much, and that was really all right. Not that I had anything against her conversation, but my ears were due for a rest and my mind had thoughts to play with. At first the thoughts centered upon the Crystal Sheldrake apartment and how I would endeavor to knock it off. I was not entirely certain that I should have said yes, and so I did a certain amount of arm-twisting on myself, building up my resolve, telling myself it was like finding money in the street.

These thoughts, while undoubtedly useful, ultimately gave way to thoughts about the comely young lady who was probing my oral cavities—which, come to think of it, sounds a damn sight more appealing that it actually was. I don't know why one would be inclined to have reprehensible fantasies about a dental hygienist but I've never been able to avoid it. Maybe it's the uniform. Nurses, stewardesses, usherettes, nuns—the male chauvinist mind will go on weaving its smarmy webs.

But Jillian Paar could have been a laundress or a street-sweeper and she'd have had the same effect on me. She was a slender slip of a girl, with straight dark brown hair cut as if with a soup bowl over her head, but clearly by someone who knew what he was doing. She had that spectacular complexion associated with the British Isles—white porcelain illuminated with a rosy glow. Her hands, unlike her employer's, were small, with narrow fingers. They did not taste boiled. Instead they smelled of spice.

She tended to lean against one while working on one's mouth. There was nothing objectionable in this. Quite the contrary, truth to tell.

So the cleaning seemed to pass in no time at all. And when it was all done and my teeth had that wonderfully shiny feel to them that they only have the first few hours after they've been cleaned, and after we'd exchanged a few pleasantries and she'd shown me for what seemed like the thousandth time the proper way to brush my teeth (and every damned dental hygienist shows you a different way, and each swears it's the *only* way) she batted an eyelash or two at me and said, "It's always good to see you, Mr. Rhodenbarr."

"Always a pleasure for me, Jillian."

"And I'm so glad to hear you're going to help Craig out and burglarize Crystal's jewels."

"Urg," I said.

I suppose I should have bailed out there and then. It was the right time for it—the plane was still in the air and I had a parachute.

But I didn't.

I wasn't happy about things. My tight-lipped dentist had managed to break security within five minutes. Presumably Jillian was his trusted confidante, and quite likely she received a good number of his confidences while both parties were in a horizontal position, an hypothesis I'd entertained earlier in light of her obvious attractions and Craig's historic predilection for diddling the help.

This didn't butter no parsnips, as my grandmother would

never have dreamed of saying. (Granny was a strict grammarian who wouldn't have said *ain't* if she had a mouthful.) As far as I was concerned, if one person knew a burglar's plan, that was awful. If two people knew, that was ten times as awful. It didn't matter if the two people were sleeping together. Hell, maybe it was *worse* if they were sleeping together. They could have a falling-out and one of them could go about blabbing resentfully.

I did take time to speak to Craig, assuring him that it would be in everybody's interest for him to give his errant tongue a Novocaine hit. He apologized and promised to be properly silent in the future, and I decided to let it go at that. I wouldn't bail out. I'd see if I couldn't fly the damn plane to safety.

Pride and greed. They'll do you in every time.

That was on a Thursday. I got out to the Hamptons for the weekend, spent half a day out on a bluefish boat, worked on my tan, sampled the bar scene, stayed at a fine old place called the Huntting Inn (spelling it with two T's was their idea), agreed with everyone that the place was a damn sight better now that the season was over, and in the course of things struck out with an impressive number of otherwise charming young ladies. By the time I was back in Manhattan where I belong, I'd eaten up a little more of my case money and was almost glad I'd decided to hit the Sheldrake residence. Not wild about it but, oh, let's say sanguine.

I spent Tuesday and Wednesday casing the joint. Wednesday night I called Craig at his East Sixty-third Street bachelor digs to get another report on Crystal's routine. I told him, not without purpose, that Saturday night sounded like the best time for me to make my move.

I didn't intend to wait until Saturday. The very next night, Thursday, I had my conversation with Miss Henrietta Tyler and cracked Crystal's crib.

And languished in her closet. And probed for a pulse in her lifeless wrist.

Four

Around ten the next morning I was spreading rhubarb preserves on a piece of whole-wheat toast. I'd bought the preserves, imported from Scotland at great expense, because I figured anything in an octagonal jar with a classy label had to be good. Now I felt an obligation to use them up even though my figuring seemed to be wrong. I had the piece of toast nicely covered and was about to cut it into triangles when the phone rang.

When I answered it Jillian Paar said, "Mr. Rhodenbarr? This is Jillian. From Dr. Craig's office?"

"Oh, hi!" I said. "Beautiful morning, isn't it? How are things in dental hygiene?"

There was a funereal pause. Then, "You haven't heard the news?"

"News?"

"I don't even know if it was in the papers. I haven't even *seen* the papers. I overslept, I just grabbed coffee and Danish on my way to the office. Craig had a nine-thirty appointment booked and he's always at the office on time and he didn't show up. I called his apartment and there was no answer, and I figured he must be on his way in, and then I had the radio on and there was a newscast."

"Jesus," I said. "What happened, Jillian?"

There was a pause and then the words came in a rush. "He

was arrested, Bernie. I know it sounds crazy but it's true. Last night someone killed Crystal. Stabbed her to death or something, and in the middle of the night the police came and arrested Craig for her murder. You didn't know about this?"

"I can't even believe it," I said. I wedged the phone between ear and shoulder so that I could quarter the toast. I didn't want it to get cold. If I have to eat rhubarb preserves I can damn well eat them on warm toast. "It wasn't in the *Times*," I added. I could have added that it wasn't in the *News* either, but that it was all over radio and television newscasts. But for some curious reason I didn't mention this.

"I don't know what to do, Bernie. I just don't know what I should do."

I took a bite of toast, chewed it thoughtfully. "I suppose the first step is to close the office and cancel his appointments for the day."

"Oh, I already did that. You know Marian, don't you? The receptionist? She's making telephone calls now. When she's done I'll send her home, and after that—"

"After that you can go home yourself."

"I suppose so. But there has to be something I can *do.*"

I ate more toast, sipped some coffee. I seemed to be developing a definite taste for the rhubarb jam. I wasn't positive I'd go running out for another jar when this one was finally finished, but I was beginning to like it. Coffee, though, was not quite the right accompaniment. A pot of strong English breakfast tea, that would be more like it. I'd have to remember next time.

"I can't believe Craig would kill her," she was saying. "She was a bitch and he hated her but I can't believe he would kill anyone. Even a rotten tramp like Crystal."

I tried to remember that Latin phrase for speaking well of the dead, then gave it up. *De mortuis ta-tum ta-tum bonum,* something along those lines.

"If only I could *talk* to him, Bernie."

"You haven't heard from him?"

"Nothing."

"What time did they pick him up?"

"They didn't say on the radio. Only that he'd been arrested

for questioning. If it was just a matter of questioning they wouldn't have had to arrest him, would they?"

"Probably not." I paused, chewed rhubarb-laden toast, considered. "When was Crystal killed? Did they happen to say?"

"I think they said the body was discovered shortly after midnight."

"Well, it's hard to say when they would have gotten around to picking Craig up. They might have questioned him without charging him for a while. He could have insisted they charge him, but he might not have thought of that. And he might not have bothered insisting on having a lawyer present. In any event, somewhere along the way he must have called an attorney. He wouldn't have a criminal lawyer but his own lawyer would have referred the case to somebody and he's almost certainly got counsel at hand by now." I thought back to my own experiences. I used a couple of mouthpieces over the years before I finally settled on Herbie Tannenbaum. He's always straight with me, I can call him at any hour, and he knows he can trust me to come up with his fee even if I don't have anything in advance. He also knows how to reach the reachable judges and how to work trade-offs with the D.A.'s people. But I somehow doubted he'd be the kind of lawyer Craig Sheldrake would wind up with.

"You could get in touch with Craig's lawyer," I added. "Find out from him how things stand."

"I don't know who he is."

"Well, maybe he'll call you. The lawyer. If only to tell you to cancel the appointments. He shouldn't take it for granted that you happened to catch the newscast."

"Why hasn't he called yet? It's almost ten-thirty!"

Because you're on the phone, I wanted to say. Instead I swallowed some food and said, "They may have waited until a decent hour before they arrested him. Don't panic, Jillian. If he's been arrested he's certainly in a safe place. If the lawyer doesn't call you sometime this afternoon, make some calls and find out where he's being held. They might even let you see him. If not, at least they'll give you the name of his attorney and you can take it from there. Don't expect Craig to call you. They'll let him call his lawyer and that's generally the extent of his phone privileges." Unless you bribe a guard, but he wouldn't know how to go about doing that.

"You don't really have anything to worry about, Jillian. Either you'll hear from the lawyer or you'll get in touch with the lawyer and either way things'll work out. If Craig's innocent—"

"Of course he's innocent!"

"—then things'll get straightened out in no time at all. They always pick up the husband when the wife gets murdered. But Crystal led a rather loose life, from what I've heard—"

"She was a slut!"

"—so it's likely there were any number of men with a good motive and opportunity to kill her, and she might even have brought home a stranger—"

"Like *Looking for Mr. Goodbar!*"

"—so I'm sure there are more suspects in this case than cockroaches on Eldridge Street, and the World's Greatest Dentist ought to be back drilling and filling in no time at all."

"Oh, I *hope* so!" She took a breath. "Can't he get out on bail? People always get out on bail, don't they?"

"Not when the charge is Murder One. There's no bail allowable in first-degree murder cases."

"That doesn't seem fair."

"Few things are." More toast, more coffee. "I think you should just sit tight, Jillian. Either where you are or at your apartment, wherever you'll be more comfortable."

"I'm scared, Bernie."

"Scared?"

"I don't know why or what of but I'm terrified. Bernie?"

"What?"

"Could you come over? It's crazy, maybe, but I don't know who else to ask. I just don't want to be alone by myself now." I hesitated, at least partly because I had some unswallowed food on my tongue, and she said, "Forget I said all that, okay? You're a busy man, I know that, and it's an imposition, and—"

"I'll be right over."

There's something to keep in mind. I didn't agree to bop on over to Craig's Central Park South office just because I have a penchant for sticking my head in the lion's mouth, or into whatever orifice the beast chooses to present to me. Nor was I making the trip because I couldn't help remembering how nice it felt when

39

Jillian leaned against me during a cleaning, or how nice her fingers tasted.

On the surface, it might look as though I had a vested interest in staying uninvolved. I was after all a burglar, and am hence regarded generally as a Highly Suspicious Person. And I was, further, no more than a dental patient and casual acquaintance of Craig Sheldrake, nor was my relationship with Jillian such that she'd be likely to turn to me before all others for solace in time of stress. Why, she'd never called me anything but Mr. Rhodenbarr until this morning. So at first glance it certainly looked as though I ought to keep a low profile.

On the other hand—and there's always another hand—whoever jammed Crystal's pump had taken a caseful of jewels along with him. I had taken to thinking of those jewels as my own, and I still thought of them as my own, and I damn well wanted to get them back.

I didn't just want the jewels, as far as that goes. The precious pretties, you may recall, were in an attaché case I'd brought into the apartment with me. I was reasonably certain no one could trace that case to me—I, after all, had stolen it in the first place. But I couldn't begin to be sure that the inside of the damn thing wasn't covered⁺ with my fingerprints. The outside was Ultrasuede and would no more take a print than Crystal Sheldrake's wrist would, but the inside was some sort of vinyl or Naugahyde, which might or might not take prints, and there was a lot of metal trim in the interior, and it wasn't at all hard to conjure up scenarios in which a cadre of cops kicked my door in and sought to learn what a case with my prints on it, loaded with Crystal's jewelry, was doing in the apartment of a murder suspect.

So if they caught him I might be in trouble. And if they didn't catch him he'd be getting away with my loot. And if there was no one to catch because the World's Greatest Dentist had indeed gone and committed the world's dumbest murder, well, that was less than super for me, too. Because in that case Craig would hand me to them on a platter. *"I was talking to him about all this jewelry she had around, see, and he seemed to be taking quite an interest, and later it dawned on me that I'd read something about him being a burglar and once being mixed up in a murder, and I never dreamed he'd actually burglarize poor Crystal's apartment—"*

I could just about write the script for him, and after the way he'd set me up a week ago, I didn't doubt he had the acting talent to read his lines properly. It might not be enough to get him out of the soup but it would certainly put me in the kettle alongside of him.

In fact, even if he wasn't guilty he might try that approach. If no other suspect turned up he could panic. Or he could have the same doubts about me that I was having about him, and he could decide I might have hit Crystal's apartment two days earlier than I said I would—which in fact I did—and that I happened to kill her accidentally in a moment of panic. He might simply have figured that our arrangement might come out so he'd better put the best possible light on it in advance.

What it came down to was that there were far too many ways that I could wind up in trouble.

And there was the fact that I liked Craig Sheldrake. When you are a patient of the World's Greatest Dentist you don't readily give him up and walk in off the street to any clown with a sign in his window advertising painless extractions. The man was taking good care of my mouth and I wanted him to carry on.

And Jillian was certainly a charming young lady. And it was much nicer to be called *Bernie* by her than *Mr. Rhodenbarr,* which had always struck me as overly formal. And her fingers did have that nice spicy taste to them, and it seemed reasonable to assume that this was characteristic of more of her than her fingers alone. Jillian was Craig's personal love interest, of course, and that was fine with me, and I had no intention of horning hornily in on another chap's romance. That's not my style. I only steal cash and inanimate objects. All the same, one needn't have designs on a young lady to find her company enjoyable. And if Craig should prove to be guilty, Jillian would be out of a job and a lover just as I would be out of a dentist, and there was no reason for us to do other than console each other.

But why build sand castles? Some evil bastard had not stopped at killing Crystal Sheldrake. He'd gone on to steal jewels I'd already stolen.

And I intended to make him pay for that.

Five

"You're fantastic, Bernie."

I must admit I'd had fantasies in which Jillian spoke those very words to me, and in approximately that tone of voice, but I hadn't been hanging up a telephone when it happened. I'd planned on being in a horizontal position at the time. Instead I was vertical, and I was replacing the receiver of the phone that perched on the desk of Marian the Receptionist. Marian was out for the day. Craig Sheldrake, on the other hand, was not. He was still behind bars— which was what my phone conversation had just determined.

A few other calls had revealed a few other things. Craig's regular attorney was a man by the name of Carson Verrill, with offices somewhere downtown. Verrill had engaged a criminal lawyer named Errol Blankenship to represent Craig in this particular matter. (The choice of phrasing was that of someone in Verrill's office.) Blankenship had an office listed in the phone book on Madison Avenue in the thirties. I tried his phone and no one answered it. If he had a home phone, either his home was outside of Manhattan or the number was unlisted. I let it go. I figured he was in court or something and his secretary had decided to celebrate by taking a long lunch hour.

Craig had been arrested in his own Upper East Side apartment around six-thirty in the morning. Not many good things happen at that time of day and being arrested certainly isn't one of them. They'd let him shave and change from his pajamas into something more suitable for street wear. I hoped he'd known to wear loafers, but how many straight-arrow citizens would think of that? They don't always take your shoelaces away from you in jail, but periodically some Yo-Yo decides you look like the suicidal sort, and there you are clumping around with your shoes falling off your feet.

Well, probably that was the least of his worries.

He was in a cell now in a hostile building downtown on Centre Street. I don't suppose he was happy about it. I've never known anyone who was. I'd asked if he could have visitors and the person I talked to didn't seem to be the voice of authority on the subject. He said he thought so, but why didn't I drop around and make sure? Whatever the ruling, the last thing I wanted to do was drop around that grim establishment myself. My previous visits had not been the sort to make me anxious to return for old time's sake.

"You're fantastic, Bernie."

Actually, she didn't say it again. I'm repeating it so as to preserve the thread of this narrative. What I said in reply was that she shouldn't be silly, that I was not fantastic, and even if I did happen to be moderately sensational in certain unspecified other areas, nevertheless I'd done nothing remarkable in her presence. Yet.

"You could have made the same calls and found out the same information," I said. "You just don't have experience with this sort of thing."

"I wouldn't have had any idea what to do."

"You could have figured it out."

"And I would have gotten all rattled on the phone. I sometimes get terribly nervous. I'm not very good at talking to people. Sometimes I think there's too much silence when I'm working on a patient. They can't talk, obviously, and I just can't manage to open my mouth."

"Believe me, it's a release after Craig does his Motormouth number."

She giggled. It was a charming giggle, which surprised me about as much as that the sun had picked the East to rise in that morning. "He does talk a lot," she acknowledged, as if painfully admitting that the Liberty Bell had a crack in it. "But that's only with patients. When he's alone he's very shy and quiet."

"Well, I wouldn't expect him to talk to himself."

"Pardon me?"

"Everybody's quiet when they're alone."

She thought about it, then blushed prettily. I'd come to think of that as a lost art. "I meant he's quiet when he's alone with me."

"I knew what you meant."

"Oh."

"I was being a smart-ass. Sorry."

"Oh, that's all right. I just—my mind's not working too brilliantly this morning. I wonder what I should do. Do you think I can go see Craig?"

"I don't know whether or not he can have visitors. You could go down there and find out, but I think it would be a good idea for us to learn a little more about what's going on first. If we had a better idea of just how good a case they've got against Craig, we might be in a better position to figure out what to do next."

"Do you think they've got a good case?"

I shrugged. "Hard to say. It would help if he has an alibi for last night, but I guess if he had a good one he'd be back on the street by now. I, uh, gather he wasn't with you?"

She blushed again. I guess there was no avoiding it. "No," she said. "We had dinner together last night but then we each had some things to do so we went our separate ways. I guess it was about nine o'clock that I saw him last. I went home and so did he."

"Uh-huh."

"Oh!" She brightened. "I talked to him before I went to bed. It was during the Carson show, I remember that. It wasn't much of a conversation, we just said goodnight to each other, but he was home then. Would that help give him an alibi?"

"Did you call him?"

"He called me."

"Then it wouldn't help his alibi a whole lot. You've only got his word as to where he was when he called you. And the police are likely to take the position that a murderer wouldn't draw the line at lying to a pretty lady."

She started to say something, then gnawed a little scarlet

lipstick from her lower lip. It was a becoming shade and a most attractive lower lip. I wouldn't have minded gnawing it myself.

"Bernie? You don't think he did it, do you?"

"I'm pretty certain he didn't."

"Why?"

I had a reason but I preferred to keep it to myself. "Because of the kind of guy he is," I said instead, and that was evidently just what she wanted to hear. She started enlarging on the topic of Craig Sheldrake, World's Greatest Guy, and I'll be damned if she didn't make him sound like someone I'd have really liked to meet.

I decided to change the subject. "The fact that we know he's innocent doesn't do him much good," I said, by way of transition. "The cops have to know he's innocent, and the easiest way for that to happen is if they've got someone else they know is guilty. Unless you're on the Orient Express, one murderer per corpse is all anybody could possibly ask for."

"Do you mean we should try to solve the crime ourselves?"

Did I? "Well, I wouldn't go that far," I said, backpedaling. "But I wish I knew more than I do. I'd like to know just when the murder was committed, and I'd like to know what men Crystal was involved with lately, and where all of them were when somebody was busy killing her. And I'd like to know if anybody had a particularly strong reason for wanting her dead. Craig had a ton of reasons, and you and I know that and so does the long arm of the law, but a woman who led as active a life as Crystal Sheldrake did must have made a few enemies along the way. Maybe some lover of hers had a jealous wife or girl friend. There's a whole world of possibilities out there and I hardly know where we should start."

She looked at me. "I'm so glad I called you, Bernie."

"Well, I don't know how much help I can really be—"

"I'm really so glad." Her eyes did a little number, and then suddenly her forehead crinkled up and her gaze narrowed. "I just thought of something," she said. "You were going to burglarize Crystal's apartment on Saturday night, weren't you? Imagine if the killer had picked that time to strike!"

Let's imagine no such thing, Jillian. "But Crystal was home last night," I reminded her, carefully shifting her gears and pointing her in a safer direction. "I would never have gone in if she was home."

"Oh. Of course. I just thought—"

Whatever she just thought will be forever unrecorded because she didn't get to the end of the sentence. There was a brisk rat-tat-tat, a loud knock on the clouded glass panel of the outer door. "Open up in there," said a professionally authoritative voice. And added, quite unnecessarily in my opinion, "It's the police."

Jillian blanched.

I, in turn, did the only possible thing under the circumstances. Without the slightest hesitation I grabbed her by the shoulders, drew her close, and brought our mouths together in a passionate embrace.

The knock was repeated.

Well, what the hell. So was the kiss.

Six

I don't know if Jillian was nonplused, but she certainly wasn't plused. Her face held an expression somewhere between bemusement and astonishment, with pronounced overtones of shock. Have I mentioned her eyes? They were the faded blue of well-washed denim, and they were large, and I had never seen them larger.

Rat-tat-tat.

"Bernie!"

"Police. Open up there."

I was still gripping her shoulders. "I'm your boyfriend," I whispered urgently. "You're not Craig's girl, you're my girl, and that's why you happened to ask me to drop over, and we've been doing a little innocent smooching."

Her mouth made an O, her eyes showed instant comprehension, and her head bobbed in affirmation. Even as I was pointing at the door she was moving toward it. I snatched a Kleenex from the box on Marian's desk, and as the door opened to reveal a pair of plainclothes cops, I was in the process of dabbing at Jillian's scarlet lipstick.

"Sorry to interrupt you," said the taller of the two. He had bigger shoulders than most people, and very widely spaced eyes, as if while in the womb he'd toyed with the idea of becoming

47

Siamese twins and decided against it at the last minute. He did not sound at all sorry to interrupt us.

"We're police," the other one said. During the July blackout someone said *"Dark out, isn't it?"* That was as unnecessary a sentence as I've ever heard uttered, and *"We're police"* came a close second.

For one thing, they'd told us as much through the locked door. For another, they damn well looked the part. The shorter one was slender rather than broad. He had black curly hair and a small, inexpertly trimmed black mustache, and no Hollywood casting director would pick him for a cop. He looked more like the member of the gang who turns stool pigeon in the second-to-last reel. But standing there in front of us he looked like a cop and so did the one with all the shoulders. Maybe it's the stance, maybe it's the facial expression, maybe it's just some aspect of the inner self they manage to project, but cops all look like cops.

This pair introduced themselves. The block of granite was Todras, the stoat was Nyswander. Todras was a detective and Nyswander was a patrolman, and if they had first names they were keeping them a secret. We furnished our names, first and last, and Todras asked Jillian to spell her first name. She did, and Nyswander wrote all this down in a little dog-eared notebook. Todras asked Jillian what people called her for short and she said they didn't.

"Well, it's just routine," Todras said. He seemed to be the natural leader of the two, the offensive guard clearing a path for Nyswander to weasel through. "I guess you heard about your boss, Miss Paar."

"There was something on the radio."

"Yeah, well, I'm afraid he's gonna have his hands full for awhile now. You got the office closed up, I see. You call around and cancel his appointments yet?"

"For the rest of the day."

The two of them exchanged glances. "Maybe you should cancel them for the rest of the month," Nyswander suggested.

"Or the rest of the year."

"Yeah, because it really looks as though he stepped in it this time."

"Maybe you better close the office for good," Todras said.

"Maybe you should."

"And find somebody else to work for."

"Somebody who figures divorce is enough and stops short of murder."

"Or someone who when he kills a former spouse finds a way to get away with it."

"Yeah, that's the idea."

"Right."

It was really something, the way the lines came back and forth from the two of them. It was as though they had a vaudeville act they were working on, and they wanted to break it in in the smaller rooms before they took it on the road. We were a sort of warm-up audience, and they were making the most of us.

Jillian didn't seem to think they were all that hysterical. Her lower lip, which now carried less than its usual quantity of lipstick, trembled slightly. Her eyes looked misty. *I'm your boyfriend,* I thought, trying to beam the thought her way. *Craig's just your boss. And don't for God's sake call him Craig.*

"I can't believe it," she said.

"Believe it, Miss Paar."

"Right," came the echo from Nyswander.

"But he wouldn't do something like that."

"You never know," Todras said.

"They'll fool you every time," said Nyswander.

"But Dr. Sheldrake couldn't kill anyone!"

"He didn't kill just anyone," Todras said.

"He killed somebody specific," Nyswander said.

"Namely his wife."

"Which is pretty specific."

Jillian frowned and her lip quivered again. I had to admire the way she was using that lip-quiver. Maybe it was real, maybe she wasn't even conscious of it, but she was fitting it into a generally effective act. It might not stun 'em in Peoria the way Todras & Nyswander might, but she got her point across.

"He's such a good man to work for," she said.

"Been working for him long, Miss Paar?"

"Quite a while. That's how I met Bernie. Mr. Rhodenbarr."

"You met Mr. Rhodenbarr here through the doc?"

She nodded. "He was a patient of the doctor's. And we met here and started seeing each other."

"And I suppose you had an appointment for some more dental work this morning. That right, Mr. Rhodenbarr?"

It wasn't right. Tempting, perhaps, but not right, and if they checked the appointment book they'd know as much. Why tell an obvious lie when a less obvious one will do?

"No," I said. "Miss Paar called me and I was able to get over to comfort her. She was anxious and didn't want to be here alone."

They nodded to each other and Nyswander wrote something down. The time and temperature, perhaps.

"I guess you been a patient of the doc's for some time, Mr. Rhodenbarr."

"A couple of years now."

"Ever meet his former wife?"

Well, we were never formally introduced. "No," I said. "I don't think so."

"She was his nurse before they got married, wasn't she?"

"His hygienist," Jillian corrected. The two of them stared at her. I said that I understood Mrs. Sheldrake had retired upon marrying her employer, and that by the time I became his patient she was no longer working at the office.

"Nice deal," Nyswander said. "You marry the boss, that's even better'n marrying the boss's daughter."

"Unless the boss kills you," Todras suggested.

The conversation drifted on in this fashion. I slipped in a tentative question now and again of the sort they could have fun doing macabre Smith-and-Dale routines with, and I managed to pick up an item here and an item there.

Item: The Medical Examiner had fixed the time of death at somewhere between midnight and one in the morning. Now you know and I know that Crystal Sheldrake died at 10:49, eleven minutes of eleven, but I couldn't find a way to supply that bit of information.

Item: There were no signs of forced entry, no indication that anything had been removed from the apartment, and everything pointed to the supposition that Crystal had admitted her killer herself. Since she was rather informally attired, even to the bathing cap on her head, it was logical to suppose that the murderer was a close acquaintance at the very least.

No argument there. No signs of forced entry, certainly, because when I bamboozle the tumblers of a lock I don't leave tracks. No indication of burglary if only because there was no mess, no drawers turned inside-out, none of the signals left behind by either an amateur at the game or a pro in a hurry. Whoever killed Crystal might well have left the apartment looking as though the Hell's Angels had sublet it for a month, but I'd made things uncommonly easy for him, gathering all the loot in advance of his call and packing it up for him. God, that rankled!

Item: Craig couldn't account for his time while his ex-wife was getting herself murdered. If he'd mentioned anything about having dinner with Jillian, the news didn't seem to have found its way to Todras & Nyswander. It would eventually, of course, and sooner or later they'd know Jillian was the boss's girlfriend and I was nothing more than your friendly neighborhood burglar. Which would, sooner or later, constitute a problem, a thorn in the side, a pain in the neck. But not yet, thank you. Meanwhile, Craig was telling them that he'd spent a quiet evening at home. A lot of people spend a lot of their evenings quietly at home, but those are the hardest sort of evenings to prove.

Item: Someone, some neighbor I supposed, had seen a man answering Craig's description leaving the Gramercy building at around the time the murder was supposed to have been committed. I couldn't tell just what time the person had been seen, or whether he'd been leaving merely the building or the specific apartment, or just who had seen him or just how certain the witness was about the time and the identification. Someone or anyone could have spotted the man who'd made love to Crystal, or the man who killed her, or even Bernard Rhodenbarr himself, beating a hasty retreat from the premises after the horse was stolen.

Or it could have been Craig. All I knew about the killer was he had two feet and he didn't talk much. If Gary Cooper were still alive he could have done it. Maybe it was Marcel Marceau. Maybe it was Craig, uncharacteristically silent.

"Wondered if we could just go into the office," Todras said. And when Jillian explained that that's where we were, in the office, he said, "Well, I don't know the name for it, maybe. The room where he does what he does."

"I beg your pardon?"

"With the chair that goes back," Nyswander said.

"And all the drills."

"And the instruments, those cute little mirrors on the ends of sticks, and the things for picking the crud out from underneath your gums."

"Oh, right," Todras said, smiling at the memory. His own teeth were large and white and even, like the snow when Good King Wenceslas looked out. (That's not exactly right, but you must know what I mean.) His wide-set eyes gleamed like high-beamed headlights over the grillwork of his smile. "And that slurpy thing that sucks up all your spit. Don't forget the slurpy thing."

"That's Mr. Thirsty," I said.

"Huh?"

Jillian led us to the room where Craig did his handiwork, solving people's problems and sending them out to do battle with tough steaks and nougat-centered chocolates. The two cops amused themselves by tilting the chair to and fro and making Dr. Kronkheit passes at each other with the drill, but then they got down to serious business and opened the cabinet with the drawers of steel implements.

"Now these here are interesting," little Nyswander said, holding a nasty little pick at arm's length. "What's this called, anyway?"

Jillian told him it was a pick for scraping tartar from the teeth. He nodded and said it must be important to do that, huh? She said it was vital; otherwise you got irritation and bone erosion and periodontal disease, and you wound up without any teeth. "People think cavities are the big thing," she explained, "but your teeth can be in perfect shape and you'll lose them anyway because of the gums."

"Those teeth are beauties," Todras said heartily, "but I'm afraid those gums have to come out."

We all laughed it up over that one. Nyswander and Todras took turns holding up implements and wanting to know what they were. This one was another pick, that one was a dental scalpel, and there were no end of others, the names and functions of which have mercifully slipped my mind.

"All these gizmos," Todras said, "there's a basic similarity, right? Like they're all part of a set, but instead of being in a case or something so you can be sure they're all here, they're just sort of lined up in the drawer. The doc buy 'em all in a set or something?"

"You can buy them in sets."

"Is that what he did?"

Jillian shrugged. "I wouldn't know. He had the office set up a good many years before I came to work for him. Of course the individual implements are available singly. These are fine-quality steel, but accidents happen. Picks drop and get bent. Scalpels get nicks. And we keep several of each implement on hand because you have to have the right tool for the job. I'm the hygienist, I don't handle paperwork, but I know we reorder individual items from time to time."

"But they're all the same," Nyswander said.

"Oh, they may look it, but the picks will be angled in slightly different ways, or—"

She stopped because he was shaking his head, but it was Todras who spoke. "They all have these six-sided handles," he said. "They all come from the same manufacturer is what he means."

"Oh. Yes, that's right."

"Who's the manufacturer, Miss Paar? You happen to know?"

"Celniker Dental and Optical Supply."

"You want to spell that, Miss Paar?" She did, and Nyswander wrote something in his notebook, capped his pen, turned a page. While he was doing this Todras brought a large hand out of his pocket and opened it to disclose yet another dental implement. It looked to me quite like the one Jillian had identified as a dental scalpel. I'd had something similar in appearance once, though undoubtedly inferior in quality. It had been part of an X-acto knife kit I had as a boy, and I'd used it to whittle sad little wingless birds from balsa blocks.

"You recognize this, Miss Paar?"

"It's a dental scalpel. Why?"

"One of yours?"

"I don't know. It's possible."

"You wouldn't know how many of this model the doc happens to have on hand?"

"I wouldn't have any idea. Quite a few, obviously."

"He ever carry them with him when he leaves the office?"

53

"Whatever for?"

Again they exchanged presumably meaningful glances.

"We found this one in Crystal Sheldrake's apartment," Nyswander said.

"Actually it was some other cop found it. He's using 'we' in the departmental sense."

"Actually it was found in Crystal Sheldrake herself."

"Actually it was in her heart."

"Actually," said Todras (or perhaps it was Nyswander), "this pretty much frosts the cupcake, don't it? Looks to me like your boss is up every creek in town."

It rattled Jillian. It didn't do a thing to me or for me, as I'd seen that hexagonal handle protruding from between Crystal's breasts while I was fumbling mindlessly for a pulse. I'd more or less known it would turn out to be one of Craig's tools, or a reasonable facsimile thereof, and I'd even toyed with the idea of carrying it off with me.

But there had been abundant reasons for not doing so. The most obvious one was that it would have been just my luck to pocket the deadly device and walk straight into the arms of a cop. It's bad enough when they catch you with burglar's tools. When you're carrying murderer's tools as well they take a dim view indeed.

Besides, as far as I was concerned the scalpel proved Craig was innocent, not guilty, and that someone had only succeeded in setting up the world's clumsiest framing job. Why would Craig use a dental scalpel to kill his wife, knowing it would point immediately to him? And why, if he did have a sufficient lapse of taste and sense to do so, would he leave the scalpel sticking out of her instead of retrieving it and carrying it away with him? Whatever line they took officially, the cops would have to reason along these lines themselves sooner or later, whereas if I had removed the scalpel and some brilliant lab work had later proved that a dental scalpel had inflicted the wound, well, then Craig would really be in a bind.

So I'd left it there, and now I was doing my best to appear as though I was seeing it for the first time. "Gee," I said, mouth agape. "That was the murder weapon?"

"You bet it was," Todras said.

"Plunged right into her heart," Nyswander added. "That's a murder weapon, all right."

"Death musta been instant."

"Hardly any bleeding. No muss, no fuss, no bother."

"Gee," I said.

Jillian was on the edge of hysteria, and I was hoping she wouldn't overreact. It was logical to assume she'd be shocked at the idea of her boss committing murder, but if their relationship was just that of dentist and hygienist there was a limit to the extent of her shock.

"I just can't believe it," she was saying. She reached out her hand to touch the scalpel, then drew back at the last moment, her fingertips just avoiding contact with the bright metal. Todras smiled fiercely and returned the scalpel to his pocket, while Nyswander drew a manilla envelope from his inside jacket pocket and commenced selecting other dental scalpels from a tray of implements. He put four or five of them into the envelope, licked the flap, sealed it, and wrote something on its outside.

Jillian asked him what he was doing. "Evidence," he said.

"The D.A.'ll want to show how the doc's got other scalpels the same size and shape as the murder weapon. You get a good look at it, Miss Paar? Maybe there's something about it, some nick or scratch you'll recognize."

"I saw it. I can't identify it, if that's what you mean. They all look alike."

"Might notice something if you give it a close look. Todras, let Miss Paar here have another look at it, huh?"

Jillian didn't much want to look at it. But she forced herself, and after a careful glance announced that there was nothing specifically familiar about the instrument, that it seemed identical to ones they used in the office. But, she added, dentists all over the country used Celniker tools, they were very common, and a search of the offices of dentists throughout New York would turn up thousands of them.

Nyswander said he was sure that was true but that only one dentist had a clear motive for killing Crystal Sheldrake.

"But he cared for her," she said. "He was hoping to get back together with her again. I don't think he ever stopped loving her."

The cops looked at each other, and I couldn't say I blamed

them. I don't know what had prompted her to start off in this direction but the cops dutifully followed it up, questioning her about this desire of Craig's for a reconciliation. Then, after she'd improvised reasonably well, Todras took the wind out of her sails by explaining that this just furnished Craig with yet another motive for murder. "He wanted to get back together," he said, "and she spurned him, so he killed her out of love."

" 'Each man kills the thing he loves,' " Nyswander quoted. " 'By each let this be heard. The coward does it with a kiss. The brave man with a sword.' And the dentist with a scalpel."

"Pretty," Todras said.

"That's Oscar Wilde."

"I like it."

"Except that part about a dentist doing it with a scalpel. Oscar Wilde never said that."

"No kidding."

"I just put that in on my own."

"No kidding."

" 'Cause it seemed to fit."

"No kidding."

I thought Jillian was going to scream. Her hands had knotted themselves into little fists. Just hang in there, I wanted to tell her, because this comedy routine of theirs takes their minds off more important things, and in a minute they'll bow and scrape themselves offstage and out of our lives, and then we can work up an act of our own.

But I guess she wasn't listening.

"Wait a minute!"

They turned and stared at her.

"Just one damn minute! How do I know you actually brought that thing with you? That scalpel? I never saw you take it out of your pocket. Maybe you picked it up off a tray while I was looking the other way. Maybe all those things you hear about police corruption are true. Framing people and tampering with evidence and—"

They were still staring at her and at about this point she just ran out of words. Not, I'd say, a moment too soon. I wished, not for the first time in my young life, that there were a way to stop the celestial tape recorder of existence, rewind it a bit, and lay down a substitute track for the most recent past.

But you can't do that, as Omar Khayyám explained long before tape recorders. The moving finger writes and all, and dear little Jillian had just gone and given us the moving finger, all right.

"This dental scalpel," said Todras, showing it to us yet again. "This particular one wasn't found in the chest of Crystal Sheldrake, as a matter of fact. Rules of evidence and everything, we don't even carry murder weapons around with us. The actual scalpel that snuffed the lady, it's in the lab right now with a tag on it while the men in the white smocks check blood types and do all the things they do."

Jillian didn't say anything.

"The scalpel my partner's showing you," Nyswander put in, "was picked up on the way here when we stopped at Celniker Dental and Optical Supply. It's an exact twin of the murder weapon and useful for us to carry around in the course of our investigation. That's why my partner can keep it in his pocket and take it out when the spirit moves him. It's not evidence so there's no way he can be tampering with it."

Todras, grinning furiously, made the scalpel disappear again. "Just for curiosity," he said, "Maybe you'd like to tell us how you spent the evening, Miss Paar."

"How I—"

"What did you do last night? Unless you can't remember."

"Last night," Jillian said. She blinked, gnawed her lip, looked beseechingly at me. "I had dinner," she said.

"Alone?"

"With me," I put in. "You're writing this down? Why? Jillian's not a suspect, is she? I thought you had an open-and-shut case against Dr. Sheldrake."

"We do," said Todras.

"It's just routine," Nyswander added. His weasel face looked craftier than ever. "So you had dinner together?"

"Right. Honey, what was the name of that restaurant?"

"Belvedere's. But—"

"Belvedere's. Right. We must have been there until nine o'clock or thereabouts."

"And then I suppose you spent a quiet evening at home?"

"Jillian did," I said. "I headed on over to the Garden myself and watched the fights. They already started by the time I got there but I saw three or four prelim bouts and the main event. Jillian doesn't care for boxing."

"I don't like violence," Jillian said.

Todras seemed to approach me without actually moving. "I suppose," he said, "you can prove you were at the fights."

"Prove it? Why do I have to prove it?"

"Oh, just routine, Mr. Rhodenbarr. I suppose you went with a friend."

"No, I went alone."

"That a fact? But you most likely ran into somebody you knew."

I thought about it. "Well, the usual ringside crowd was there. The pimps and the dope dealers and the sports crowd. But I'm just a fan, I don't actually know any of those people except to recognize them when I see them."

"Uh-huh."

"The fellow who sat next to me, we were talking about the fighters and all, but I don't know his name and I don't even know if I'd recognize him again."

"Uh-huh."

"Anyway, why would I have to prove where I was?"

"Just routine," Nyswander said. "Then you can't—"

"*Oh,*" I said brightly. "Hell, I wonder if I have my ticket stub. I don't remember throwing it out." I looked at Jillian. "Was I wearing this jacket last night? You know, I think I was. I probably dropped the stub in the garbage, or when I was cleaning out my pockets before I went to bed. Maybe it's in a wastebasket at my apartment. I don't suppose—oh, here's something."

And, amazingly enough, I showed Nyswander an orange stub from last night's fight card at Madison Square Garden. He eyed it sullenly before passing it to Todras, who didn't seem any happier to see it, his smile notwithstanding.

The ticket stub cooled things. They didn't suspect us of anything, they knew they already had the murderer in a cell, but Jillian had irritated them and they were getting a little of their own back. They returned to a less intimidating line of questioning, just rounding out things in their notebook before moving on. I could relax now, except that you can't relax until they're out the door and gone, and they were in the process of going when Todras raised a big hand, placed it atop his big head, and scratched diligently.

"Rhodenbarr," he said. "Bernard Rhodenbarr. Now where in the hell have I heard that name before?"

"Gee," I said, "I don't know."

"What's your line of work, Bernie?"

A warning bell sounded. When they start calling you by your first name it means they've pegged you as a criminal. As long as you're a citizen in their eyes it's always Mr. Rhodenbarr, but when they call you Bernie it's time to watch out. I don't think Todras even knew what he'd said, but I heard him, and the ice was getting very thin out there.

"I'm in investments," I said. "Mutual funds, open-end real-estate trusts. Estate planning, that's the real focus of what I do."

"That a fact. Rhodenbarr, Rhodenbarr. I know that name."

"I don't know where from," I said. "Unless you grew up in the Bronx."

"How'd you know that?"

By your accent, I thought. Anybody who sounds like Penny Marshall in *Laverne and Shirley* could have grown up nowhere else. But I said, "What high school?"

"Why?"

"What school?"

"James Monroe. Why?"

"Then that explains it. Freshman English. Don't you remember Miss Rhodenbarr? Maybe she's the one who had you reading Oscar Wilde."

"She's an English teacher?"

"She was. She passed on—oh, I don't know exactly how many years ago. Little old lady with iron-gray hair and perfect posture."

"Relative of yours?"

"My dad's sister. Aunt Peg, but she'd have been Miss Margaret Rhodenbarr as far as her students were concerned,"

"Margaret Rhodenbarr."

"That's right."

He opened his notebook, and for a moment I thought he was going to write down my aunt's name, but he wound up shrugging his great shoulders and putting the book away. "Must be it," he said. "A name like that, it's distinctive, you know? Sticks in the mind and rings a bell. Maybe I wasn't in her class myself but I just have a recollection of the name."

"That's probably it."

"It woulda come to me," he said, holding the door for Nyswander. "Memory's a funny thing. You just let it find it's own path and things come to you sooner or later."

Seven

Jillian and I left the office together ten or fifteen minutes after Todras and Nyswander. We joined the lunch crowd at a coffee shop around the corner on Seventh Avenue. We had coffee and grilled-cheese sandwiches, and I wound up eating half of her sandwich along with my own.

"Crystal Sheldrake," I said between bites. "What do we know about her?"

"She's dead."

"Beside that. She was Craig's ex-wife and somebody killed her, but what else do we know about her?"

"What difference does it make, Bernie?"

"Well, she was killed for a reason," I said. "If we knew the reason we might have a shot at figuring out who did it."

"Are we going to solve the murder?"

I shrugged. "It's something to do."

But Jillian insisted it was exciting, and her blue eyes danced at the prospect. She decided we would be Nick and Nora Charles, or possibly Mr. and Mrs. North, two pairs of sleuths she had a tendency to confuse. She wanted to know how we would get started and I turned the conversation back to Crystal.

"She was a tramp, Bernie. Anybody could have killed her."

"We only have Craig's word that she was a tramp. Men tend to have strict standards when it comes to their ex-wives."

"She hung out in bars and picked up men. Maybe one of them turned out to be a homicidal maniac."

"And he just happened to have a dental scalpel in his pocket?"

"Oh." She picked up her cup, took a delicate sip of coffee. "Maybe the guy she picked up was a dentist and—but I guess most dentists don't carry scalpels around in their pockets."

"Only the ones who are homicidal maniacs in their off hours. And even if she was killed by a dentist, he wouldn't have left the scalpel sticking in her. No, somebody swiped a scalpel from the office deliberately to frame Craig for the killing. And that means the murderer wasn't a stranger and the murder wasn't a spur-of-the-moment thing. It was planned, and the killer was someone with a motive, someone who was involved in Crystal Sheldrake's life. Which means we ought to learn something about that life."

"How?"

"Good question. Do you want some more coffee?"

"No. Bernie, maybe she kept a diary. Do women still keep diaries?"

"How would I know?"

"Or a stack of love letters. Something incriminating that would let us know who she was seeing. If you could break into her apartment—what's the matter?"

"The horse has already been stolen."

"Huh?"

"The time to break into an apartment," I said, "is before someone gets killed in it. Once a murder takes place the police become very efficient. They put seals on the doors and windows and even stake the place out now and then. And they also search whatever the killer left behind, so if there was a diary or a pile of letters, and if the killer didn't have the presence of mind to carry it away with him"—like a caseful of jewels, I thought with some rancor—"then the cops already have it. Anyway, I don't think there was a diary or a love letter in the first place."

"Why not?"

"I don't think Crystal was the type."

"But how would you know what type she was? You never even met her, did you?"

I avoided the question by catching the waitress's eye and making the usual gesture of scribbling in midair. I wondered, not for the first time, what diner had invented that bit of pantomime and how it had gone over with the first waiter who was exposed to it. Monsieur desires the pen of my aunt? *Eh bien?*

I said, "She had a family somewhere, didn't she? You could get in touch with them, pass yourself off as a friend from college."

"What college?"

"I don't remember, but you can. get that from the newspaper article, too."

"I'm younger than she was. I couldn't have been at college the same year."

"Well, nobody's going to ask your age. They'll be too overcome with grief. Anyway, you can probably do this over the phone. I just thought you could poke around the edges of her life and see if any male names come into the picture. The point is that she probably had a boy friend or two or three, and that would give us a place to start."

She thought about it. The waitress came over with the check and I got my wallet out and paid it. Jillian, frowning in concentration, didn't offer to pay her half of the check. Well, that was all right. After all, I'd polished off half her sandwich.

"Well," she said, "I'll try."

"Just make some phone calls and see what happens. Don't give your right name, of course. And you'd better stay pretty close to home in case Craig tries to get hold of you. I don't know if he'll be able to make any calls himself, but his lawyer may be getting in touch with you."

"How will I get ahold of you, Bernie?"

"I may be hard to reach. I'm in the book, B. Rhodenbarr on West Seventy-first, but I won't be hanging out there much. What I'll do, I'll call you. Is your phone listed?"

It wasn't. She searched her wallet and wrote her number and address on the back of a beautician's appointment card. Her appointment had been nine days ago with someone named Keith. I don't know whether or not she kept it.

"And you, Bernie? What'll you be doing?"

"I'll be looking for someone."

"Who?"

"I don't know. But I'll know her when I find her."

"A woman? How will you know her?"

"She'll be doing some serious drinking," I said, "in a very frivolous bar."

The bar was called the Recovery Room. The cocktail napkins had nurse cartoons all over them. The only one I remember featured a callipygian Florence Nightingale asking a leering sawbones what she should do with all these rectal thermometers. There was a list of bizarre cocktails posted. They had names like Ether Fizz and I-V Special and Post Mortem and were priced at two or three dollars a copy. Assorted props of a medical nature were displayed haphazardly on the walls—Red Cross splints, surgical masks, that sort of thing.

For all of this, the place didn't seem to be drawing a hospital crowd. It was on the first floor of a brick-front building on Irving Place a few blocks below Gramercy Park, too far west of Bellevue to be catching their staff, and the clientele looked to be composed primarily of civilians who lived or worked in the neighborhood. And it was frivolous, all right. If it had been any more frivolous it would have floated away.

Frankie's drinking, on the other hand, was certainly serious enough to keep the Recovery Room anchored in grim reality. A stinger is always a reasonably serious proposition. A brace of stingers at four o'clock on a weekday afternoon is about as serious as you can get.

I made several stops before I got to the Recovery Room. I'd started off with a stop at my own place, then cabbed down to the East Twenties and began making the rounds. A little gourmet shop on Lexington sold me a teensy-weensy bottle of imported olive oil, which I rather self-consciously opened and upended and drained around the corner. I'd read about this method of coating the old tumtum before a night of heavy drinking. I'll tell you, it wasn't the greatest taste sensation I ever experienced, and no sooner had I knocked it back than I began bar-hopping, hitting a few joints on Lexington, drifting over to Third Avenue, then doubling back and ultimately finding my way to the Recovery Room. In the course of this I had a white wine spritzer in each of several places and stayed long enough to determine that no one wanted to talk about

Crystal Sheldrake. I did run into two fellows who would have been glad to talk about baseball and one old fart who wanted to talk about Texas, but that was as much conversation as I could scrape up.

Until I met Frankie. She was a tallish woman with curly black hair and a sullen, hard-featured face, and she was sitting at the Recovery Room's bar sipping a stinger and smoking a Virginia Slim and humming a rather toneless version of "One for My Baby." I suppose she was around my age, but by nightfall she'd be a lot older. Stingers'll do that.

I somehow knew right away. It just looked like Crystal's kind of place and Frankie looked like Crystal's kind of people. I went up to the bar, ordered my spritzer from a bartender with a sad, hung-over look to him, and asked Frankie if the seat next to her was taken. This was forward of me—there were only two other customers at the bar, a pair of salesmen types playing the match game at the far end. But she didn't mind.

"Welcome aboard, brother," she said. "You can sit next to me long as you like. Just so you're not a goddamned dentist."

Aha!

She said, "I'll tell you what she was, Bernie. She was the salt of the fucking earth is what she was. Well, hell, you knew her, right?"

"Years ago."

"Years ago, right. 'Fore she was married. 'Fore she married that murdering toothpuller. I swear to God I'll never go to one of those bastards again. I don't care if every tooth I got rots in my head. The hell with it, right?"

"Right, Frankie."

"I don't have to chew anything anyway. The hell with food is what I say. If I can't drink it I don't need it. Right?"

"Right."

"Crystal was a lady. That's what she was. The woman was a fucking lady. Right?"

"You bet."

"Damn right." She crooked a finger at the bartender. "Rodge," she said. "Roger, honey, I want another of these, but let's make it plain brandy and let's cool it with the crème de menthe,

65

huh? Because it's beginning to taste like Lavoris and I don't want to be reminded of dentists. Got that?"

"Got it," Roger said, and took her glass away and hauled out a clean one. "Brandy, right? Brandy rocks?"

"Brandy no rocks. Ice cracks your stomach. Also it shrinks your blood vessels, the veins and the arteries. And the crème de menthe gives you diabetes. I oughta stay away from stingers, but they're my downfall. Bernie, you don't want to be drinking those spritzers all night."

"I don't?"

"First of all, the soda water's bad for you. The bubbles get into your veins and give you the bends, same as the sandhogs get when they don't go through decompression chambers. It's a well-known fact."

"I never heard that, Frankie."

"Well, you know it now. Plus the wine rots your blood. It's made out of grapes and the enzymes from the grapes are what screw you up."

"Brandy's made from grapes."

She gave me a look. "Yeah," she said, "but it's distilled. That purifies it."

"Oh."

"You want to get rid of that spritzer before it ruins your health. Have something else."

"Maybe a glass of water for now."

She looked horrified. "Water? In this town? You ever see blow-up photos of what comes out of the tap in New York City? My God, they got these fucking microscopic worms in New York water. You drink water without alcohol in it, you're just asking for trouble."

"Oh."

"Let me look at you, Bernie." Her eyes, light brown with a green cast to them, fought to focus on mine. "Scotch," she said authoritatively. "Cutty rocks. Rodge, sugar, bring Bernie here a Cutty Sark on the rocks."

"I don't know, Frankie."

"Jesus," she said, "just shut up and drink it. You're gonna drink to Crystal's memory with a glass of wormy water? What are you, crazy? Just shut up and drink your scotch."

"Now take Dennis here," Frankie said. "Dennis was crazy about Crystal. Weren't you, Dennis?"

"She was an ace-high broad," Dennis said.

"Everybody loved her, right?"

"Lit up the joint when she walked in the door," Dennis said. "No question about it. Now she's deader'n Kelsey's nuts and ain't it a hell of a thing? The husband, right?"

"A dentist."

"Wha'd he do, shoot her?"

"Stabbed her."

"A hell of a thing," Dennis said.

We had left the Recovery Room a drink or two ago at Frankie's insistence and had moved around the corner to Joan's Joynt, a smaller and less brightly lit place, and there we had met up with Dennis, a thickly built man who owned a parking garage on Third Avenue. Dennis was drinking Irish whiskey with small beer chasers, Frankie was staying with straight Cognac, and I was following orders and lapping up the Cutty Sark on the rocks. I was by no means convinced of the wisdom of this course of action, but with each succeeding drink it seemed to make more sense. And I kept reminding myself of the little bottle of olive oil I had swigged earlier. I imagined the oil coating my stomach so that the Cutty Sark couldn't be absorbed. Drink after drink would slide down my throat, hit the greased stomach and be whisked on past it into the intestine before it knew what hit it.

And yet it did seem as though a wee bit of the alcohol was getting into the old bloodstream after all . . .

"Another round," Dennis was saying heartily. "And have something for yourself, Jimbo. And that's another brandy for Frankie here, and another Cutty for my friend Bernie."

"Oh, I don't—"

"Hey, I'm buying, Bernie. When Dennis buys, everybody drinks."

So Dennis bought and everybody drank.

In the Hen's Tooth, Frankie said, "Bernie, want you to meet Charlie and Hilda. This is Bernie."

"The name's Jack," Charlie said. "Frankie, you got this obsession my name's Charlie. You know damn well it's Jack."

"The hell," Frankie said. "Same thing, isn't it?"

Hilda said, "Pleasure to meetcha, Bernie. You an insurance man like everybody else?"

"He's no fucking dentist," Frankie said.

"I'm a burglar," said six or seven Cutty Rockses.

"A what?"

"A cat burglar."

"That a fact," said someone. Jack or Charlie, I suppose. Perhaps it was Dennis.

"What do you do with them?" Hilda wanted to know.

"Do with what?"

"The cats."

"He holds 'em for ransom."

"There any money in it?"

"Jesus, lookit who's askin' if there's any money in pussy."

"Oh, you're terrible," said Hilda, clearly delighted. "You're an awful man."

"No, seriously," Charlie/Jack said. "What do you do, Bernie?"

"I'm in investments," I said.

"Terrific."

"Thank God my ex was an accountant," Hilda said. "I never thought I'd hear myself saying that and just listen to me. But you never have to worry about an accountant killing you."

"I don't know," Dennis said. "My experience is they nickel and dime you to death."

"But they don't stab you."

"You're better off with a stabbing. Get the damn thing over and done with. People look at a parking garage, all they see is that money coming in every day. They don't see the constant headaches. Those kids you gotta hire, they scrape a fender and you hear about it, believe me. Nobody appreciates the amount of mental strain in a parking garage."

Hilda put a hand on his arm. "They think you got it easy," she said, "but it's not that easy, Dennis."

"Damn right. And then they wonder why a man drinks. A

business like mine and a wife like mine and they wonder why a man needs to unwind a little at the end of the day."

"You're a hell of a guy, Dennis."

I excused myself to make a phone call, but by the time I got to the phone I couldn't remember who I'd intended to call. I went to the men's room instead. There were a lot of girl's names and phone numbers written over the urinal but I didn't notice Crystal's. I thought of dialing one of the numbers just to see what would happen. I decided it was not the sort of thought to which a sober man is given.

When I got back to the bar Charlie/Jack was ordering another round. "Almost forgot you," he said to me. "Cutty on the rocks, right?"

"Er," I said.

"Hey, Bernie," Frankie said. "You okay? You look a little green around the gills."

"It's the olive oil."

"Huh?"

"It's nothing," I said, and reached for my drink.

Eight

There were a lot of bars, a lot of conversations, a lot of people threading their separate ways in and out of my awareness. My awareness, come to think of it, was doing some threading of its own. I kept going in and out of gray stages, as if I were in a car driving through patches of fog.

Then all at once I was walking, and for the first time all night I was by myself. I'd finally lost Frankie, who'd been with me ever since the Recovery Room. I was walking, and there in front of me was Gramercy Park. I went over to the iron gate and held onto it. Not exactly for support, but it did seem like a good idea.

The park was empty, at least as much of it as I could see. I thought of picking the lock and letting myself in. I wasn't carrying anything cumbersome like a pry bar, but I did have my usual ring of picks and probes and that was sufficient to get me inside, safe from dogs and strangers. I could stretch out on a nice comfortable green bench and close my eyes and count Cutties sailing over rocks, and in only a matter of time I'd be . . . what?

Under arrest, in all likelihood. They take a dim view of bums passing out in Gramercy Park. It's frowned on.

I maintained my grip on the gate, which did seem to be swaying, although I knew it wasn't. A jogger ran by—or a runner jogged by, or what you will. Perhaps he was the same one who'd run or jogged around the park while I'd been talking with Miss Whatserface. Taylor? Tyler? No matter. No matter whether it was the same jogger or not, either. What was it she'd said about jogging? "Nothing that appears so ridiculous can possibly be good for you."

I thought about that, and thought too that I probably looked fairly ridiculous myself, clinging desperately to an iron gate as I was. And while I thought this the jogger circled round again, his canvas-clad feet tapping away at the concrete. Hadn't taken him long to circle the park, had it? Or was it a different jogger? Or had something bizarre happened to my sense of time?

I watched him jog away. "Carry on," I said, aloud or otherwise, I'm afraid I'll never know. "Just so you don't do it in the street and frighten the horses."

Then I was in a cab, and I must have given the driver my address because the next thing I knew we were waiting for a traffic light on West End Avenue a block below my apartment. "This is good enough," I told the driver. "I'll walk the rest of the way. I can use the fresh air."

"Yeah," he said. "I'll bet you can."

I paid him and tipped him and watched him drive away, and all the while I was sorting through my brain, trying to think of a snappy retort. I finally decided the best thing would be to yell, "Oh, yeah?" but I told myself he was already several blocks distant and was thus unlikely to be suitably impressed. I filled my lungs several times with reasonably fresh air and walked a block north.

I felt lousy, full of booze I hadn't wanted in the first place, my brain numb and my body shaky and my spirit sagging. But I was homing in on my own turf and there's a comfort in getting back home, even when home is an overpriced couple of rooms designed to give you a good case of the lonelies. Here, at least, I knew where I was. I could stand on the corner of Seventy-first and West End and look around and see things I recognized.

I recognized the coffee shop on the corner, for instance. I recognized the oafish Great Dane and the willowy young man who was walking or being walked by the beast. Across the street I recognized my neighbor Mrs. Hesch, the inescapable cigarette smoldering in the corner of her mouth, as she passed the doorman with a sandwich from the deli and a *Daily News* from the stand on Seventy-second Street. And I recognized the doorman, Crazy Felix, who tried so hard all his life to live up to the twin standards of his maroon uniform and his outsized mustache. And in earnest conversation with Felix I recognized Ray Kirschmann, a poor but dishonest cop whose path has crossed mine on so many occasions. And near the building's entrance I recognized a young couple who seemed to be stoned on Panamanian grass twenty hours out of twenty-four. And diagonally across the street—

Wait a minute!

I looked again at Ray Kirschmann. It was him, all right, good old Ray, and what on earth was he doing in my lobby, talking to my doorman?

A lot of cobwebs began to clear from my mind. I didn't get struck sober but it certainly felt as though that was what had happened. I stood still for a moment, trying to figure out what was going on, and then I realized I could worry about that sort of thing when I had the time. Which I didn't just now.

I moved back across the sidewalk to the shelter of shadows, glanced back to make sure Ray hadn't taken notice of me, started to walk east on Seventy-first, keeping close to the buildings all the while, glanced back again a few times to see if there were any other cops around, remainded myself that this business of glancing back all the time simply gave me the appearance of a suspicious character, and what with looking back in spite of this realization, ultimately stepped smack into a souvenir left on the pavement by the galumphing Great Dane or another of his ilk. I said a four-letter word, a precise description indeed of that in which I had stepped. I wiped my foot and walked onward to Broadway, and a cab came along and I hailed it.

"Where to?"

"I don't know," I said. "Drive downtown a little ways, it'll come to me." And then, while he was saying something I felt no need to attend to, I dug out my wallet and managed to find the little card she'd given me.

"My appointment's with Keith," I said. "But what good is this? It was almost two weeks ago."

"You okay, Mac?"

"No," I said. I turned the card over and frowned at what was written on it. "RH7-1802," I read. "Let's try that, all right? Drive me there."

"Mac?"

"Hmmm?"

"That's a phone number."

"It is?"

"Rhinelander seven, that's the exchange. My phone is all numbers, but some people still got letters and numbers. I think it's more classy, myself."

"I agree with you."

"But I can't drive you to a phone number."

"The address is right under it," I said, squinting. "Right under it." The letters, I did not add, were squirming around before my very eyes.

"Wanta read it to me?"

"In a minute or so," I said, "that's just what I'm going to do."

She lived in a renovated brickfront on East Eighty-fourth, just a block and a half from the river. I found her bell and rang it, not expecting anything to happen, and while I was preparing to let myself in she asked who I was via the intercom. I told her and she buzzed me in. I climbed three flights of stairs and found her waiting in the doorway, clothed in a blue velour robe and a frown.

She said, "Bernie? Are you all right?"

"No."

"You look as if—did you say you're *not* all right? What's the matter?"

"I'm drunk," I said. She stepped aside and I walked past her into a small studio apartment. A sofa had converted itself into a bed and she had evidently just emerged therefrom to let me in.

"You're drunk?"

"I'm drunk," I agreed. "I had olive oil and white wine and soda and Scotch and rocks. The soda water gave me the bends and the ice cracked my stomach."

"The ice—?"

"Cracked my stomach. It also shrinks the blood vessels, the veins and the arteries. Crème de menthe gives you diabetes but I stayed the hell away from it." I took off my tie, rolled it up, put it in my pocket. I took off my jacket, aimed it at a chair. "I don't know what the olive oil does," I said, "but I don't think it was a good idea."

"What are you doing?"

"I'm getting undressed," I said. "What does it look like I'm doing? I found out a lot about Crystal. I just hope I remember some of it in the morning. I certainly can't remember it now."

"You're taking your pants off."

"Of course I am. Oh, hell, I better take my shoes off first. I usually get the order right but I'm in rotten shape tonight. Wine's made out of grapes and it poisons the blood. Brandy's distilled so that purifies it."

"Bernie, your shoes—"

"I know," I said. "I've got a cop in my lobby and something even worse on my shoe. I know all that."

"Bernie—"

I got into bed. There was only one pillow. I took it and put my head on it and I pulled the covers over my head and closed my eyes and shut out the world.

Nine

After six or seven hours' sleep, after the fourth aspirin and the third cup of coffee, the fog began to break up and disperse. I looked over at Jillian, who sat in a sling chair balancing a coffee cup on her knee. "I'm sorry," I said, not for the first time.

"Forget it, Bernie."

"Bursting in on you like that in the middle of the night. Jumping out of my clothes and diving into your bed. What's so funny?"

"You make it sound like rape. You had too much to drink, that's all. And you needed a place to stay."

"I could have gone to a hotel. If I'd had the brains to think of it."

"You might have had trouble finding one that would rent you a room."

I lowered my eyes. "I must have been a mess."

"Well, you weren't at your best. I cleaned off your shoe, incidentally."

"God, that's something else for me to apologize for. Why do people keep dogs in the city?"

"To protect their apartments from burglars."

"That's a hell of a reason." I drank some more coffee and patted my breast pocket, looking for a cigarette. I quit a few years ago but I still reach for the pack now and then. Old habits die hard. "Say, where did you, uh, sleep last night?"

"In the chair."

"I'm really sorry."

"Bernie, stop it." She smiled, looking remarkably fresh for someone who had spent the night in a sling chair. She was wearing jeans and a powder-blue sweater and she looked sensational. I was wearing last night's outfit minus the tie and jacket. She said, "You said you found out some things about Crystal. Last night."

"Oh. Right."

"But you didn't seem to remember what they were."

"I didn't?"

"No. Or else you were just too exhausted to think straight. Do you remember now?"

It took me a few minutes. I had to sit back and close my eyes and give my memory little nudges, but in the end it came through for me. "Three men," I said. "I got most of my information from a woman named Frankie who was evidently a pretty good drinking buddy of Crystal's. Frankie was drunk when I met her and she didn't exactly sober up as the night wore on, but I think she knew what she was talking about.

"According to her, Crystal was just a girl who liked to have a good time. All she wanted out of life was a couple of drinks and a couple of laughs and the ever-popular goal of true love."

"Plus a million dollars worth of jewelry."

"Frankie didn't mention jewelry. Maybe Crystal didn't wear much when she went bar-hopping. Anyway, the impression I got from her was that Crystal didn't make a policy of picking up strangers. She went to the bars primarily for the booze and the small talk. Now and then she got half in the bag and went home with somebody new at the end of the evening, but as a general rule she limited herself to three guys."

"And one of them killed her?"

I shrugged. "It's a reasonable assumption. At any rate, they were the three men in her life." I picked up that morning's *Daily News,* tapped the story we'd read. The Medical Examiner had told them what I'd already known. "Somebody was intimate with her the evening she was killed. Either the killer or someone else. And that would have been early in the evening so it's not likely that she'd already gotten smashed and dragged a stranger home with her."

"I don't know, Bernie. According to Craig, she was more of a tramp than this Frankie seemed to think she was."

"Well, Craig was prejudiced. He was paying alimony."

"That's true. Do you know who the three men are?"

I nodded. "This is where it gets tricky. I had trouble questioning Frankie because I couldn't let her think I was too interested or she'd wonder what it was all about. Then as the night wore on I was too smashed to do a good job as Mr. District Attorney. And I'm not sure how much Frankie really knew about Crystal's boyfriends. I think two of them were married."

"Almost everybody is."

"Really? I thought everybody was divorced. But two of Crystal's three were married." Including, I thought, the one who'd been rolling around with her while I'd languored in her closet, the one who had to hurry on home to What's-Her-Name. "One of them's a lawyer. Frankie referred to him as the Legal Beagle when she wasn't calling him Snoopy. I think his first name may be John."

"You think it may?"

"Un-huh. Frankie did an Ed MacMahon imitation a couple of times in reference to him. 'And now, heeeeeeeere's Johnny!' So I assume that's his name."

"A married lawyer named Johnny."

"Right."

"That sure narrows it down."

"Doesn't it? Married Boyfriend Number Two is a little easier to get a line on. He's a painter and his name is Grabow."

"His last name?"

"I suppose so. I suppose he has a first name to go with it. Unless he's very artsy and he just uses the ole name. Frankie was pretty vague on the subject of Grabow."

"It sounds to me as though she was pretty vague about everything."

"Well, she was, but I don't think she ever met Grabow. At least that's the impression I got. She saw a lot of the Legal Beagle because Crystal used to drink with him in the bars. I gather Frankie found him amusing, but I don't know whether she laughed with him or at him. But I have the feeling all she knew about

Grabow was what Crystal told her, and that may not have amounted to very much."

"What about the third man?"

"He's easy. Maybe because he's not married, or at least I don't think he's married, which would mean he'd have nothing to hide. Anyway, Frankie knows him. His name is Knobby and he tends bar at Spyder's Parlor. That's one of the places I hit last night."

"So you met him?"

"No. We went there looking for him but he'd switched shifts with Lloyd."

"Who's Lloyd?"

"The guy who was tending bar at Spyder's Parlor last night. I'll tell you one thing, he pours a hell of a drink. I don't know Knobby's last name. I don't know Frankie's last name, come to think of it, or anybody's last name. None of the people I met last night had last names. But I don't suppose it'll be hard to find Knobby, not if he hangs onto his job."

"I wonder why he didn't work last night."

"Beats me. I gather the bartenders switch shifts with each other all the time. Maybe there was something on television Knobby didn't want to miss. Or maybe he had to sit up washing Crystal's blood out of his official Spyder's Parlor T-shirt. Not really, because there wasn't any blood to speak of."

"How do you know that, Bernie?"

Brilliant. "She was stabbed in the heart," I said. "So there wouldn't have been much bleeding."

"Oh."

"So here's what we've got," I said, changing the subject back where it belonged. "The Legal Beagle, Grabow the Artist, and Knobby the Bartender. I think we'll have to concentrate on the three of them for the time being."

"How?"

"Well, we can find out who they are. That would be a start."

"And then what?"

And then I could see who had the jewels, but I couldn't tell Jillian that. She didn't know anything about my Ultrasuede attaché case filled with twice-stolen pretties, nor did she know B. G. Rhodenbarr had been on the premises when Crystal got hers.

"And then," I said, "we can see if one of them had a reason

for killing Crystal, and if there was any link between any of them and Craig, because the killer didn't just happen to turn up with a dental scalpel because the local hardware store was fresh out of javelins. If it turns out that Grabow's got a partial plate that Craig made for him, or—God, I'm stupid today. You're really seeing me at my worst, Jillian. Drunk last night and hungover this morning. I've got a brain underneath it all, honest I do. A small one, but it's stood me in good stead over the years."

"What are you talking about?"

"Your files. Well, Craig's files, actually. Knobby and Grabow and the Beagle. Craig has a record of everyone he's seen professionally, doesn't he? Grabow'll be a cinch if he was ever a patient, unless Frankie got his name wrong. Knobby'll be harder until I learn what his legal name is, but that shouldn't take long and then you can see if there's any connection between him and Craig. As far as Johnny the Lawyer is concerned, well, there we've got a problem. I don't suppose you have your patients listed by occupation."

She shook her head. "There's blanks for business address and employer on the chart, but when they're self-employed they don't usually specify what they're self-employed at. I know what I could do."

"What?"

"I could go through and pull all the Johns who aren't obviously something other than lawyers, and then I can check the ones who are left against the listings of attorneys in the Yellow Pages. Not all lawyers are listed, of course. I guess most of them aren't. But does it sound as though it might be worthwhile?"

"It sounds like a long shot. And a lot of hard work."

"I know."

"But every once in a while somebody sifts through a haystack and actually comes up with a needle. If you don't mind taking the time—"

"I don't have anything else to do. And it'll at least give me the feeling that I'm doing something to help."

"You're harboring a fugitive," I said. "That's something."

"Do you really think you're a fugitive? Just because you recognized a policeman in your lobby doesn't mean he was there waiting for you. He might have been checking on some other tenant."

"Mrs. Hesch, say. Maybe he came to arrest her for smoking in the elevator."

"But he wasn't even one of the cops we saw before, Bernie. Why would he be the one to go looking for you? I could understand if it was . . . I forget their names."

"Todras and Nyswander. Todras was the block of granite with the menacing smile. Nyswander was Wilbur the Weasel."

"Well, if they were waiting for you, then you'd have something to worry about. But I don't think—who's that?"

The doorbell sounded again, right on cue.

I said, "I came here last night around one. I left about an hour ago. You don't know anything about my being a burglar. I never really talk much about my work and we haven't been going together that long. You've been seeing other men beside me, see, although you haven't let me know that."

"Bernie, I—"

"Pay attention. You can answer the bell in a minute. They're downstairs and they're not about to kick the door in. You're Craig's girl friend, it might even be a good idea to volunteer that, but you like to play the field a bit and neither Craig nor I knows you're seeing the other one. You'd better use the intercom now. I'll have time to get out before any New York cop can drag his ass up three flights of stairs."

She walked to the wall, depressed the switch to activate the intercom. "Yes?" she said. "Who is it?"

"Police officers."

She looked at me. I nodded and she poked the buzzer to let them in. I went to the door, opened it, put one foot out into the hallway. "It's official," I said, "you've been harboring a fugitive, but you didn't know it so it's not your fault. For that matter, nobody told me I was a fugitive. I lied to the cops about my line of work, but why not, since I didn't want *you* to know about it? I think we'll both be all right. I'll get in touch with you later, either here or at the office. Don't forget to go through the files."

"Bernie—"

"No time," I said, and blew her a kiss and scampered.

. . .

I had ample time to climb one flight of stairs while Todras and Nyswander were climbing three. I loitered on the top step and listened while their feet led them to Jillian's door. They knocked. The door opened. They entered. The door closed. I gave them a minute to get comfortable, then descended a flight and stood beside the door, listening. I heard voices but couldn't make them out. I could tell there were two of them, though, and I'd heard both pairs of feet on the stairs, and I didn't want to hang around until one of them got psychic and yanked the door open. I went down three more flights of stairs and took my tie out of my pocket and put it right back when I saw how wrinkled it was.

The sun seemed brighter than it had to be. I blinked at it, momentarily uncertain, and a voice said, "If it ain't my old pal Bernie."

Ray Kirschmann, the best cop money can buy, stood with his abundant backside resting upon the fender of a blue-and-white police cruiser. He had a lazy smile on his broad face. A smile of insupportable smugness.

I said, "Oh, hell, Ray. Long time no see."

"Been ages, hasn't it?" He drew the passenger door open, nodded at the seat. "Hop in," he said. "We'll have us a ride on a beautiful morning like this. It's no kind of a day to be inside, like in a cell or anything like that. Hop in, Bern."

I hopped.

Ten

Every block in New York sports several fire hydrants spaced at intervals along the sidewalk. These have been installed so that the police won't have to circle the block looking for a parking space. Ray pulled away from one of them and told me I'd just missed a couple of friends of his. "A couple of fellows in plainclothes," he said. "Myself, I'm happy wearin' the uniform. These two, you musta missed each other by a whisker. Maybe they were in the elevator while you was on the stairs."

"There's no elevator."

"That a fact? Just plain bad luck you didn't run into them, Bernie. But I guess you made their acquaintance yesterday. Here they missed you, and now they'll come downstairs and find that I took a powder my own self. Not that they'll be sorry to see me gone. They come here on their own, you know, in their own blue-and-white, and I tagged along and I had the feelin' they wanted to tell me to get lost. You take a cop and put a business suit on him and he develops an attitude, you know what I mean? All of a sudden he thinks he's a member of the human race and not your ordinary flatfoot. You want a smoke, Bernie?"

"I quit a few years ago."

"Good for you. That's strength of character is what it is. I'd quit myself if I had the will power. What's all this crap about your aunt teaching school in the Bronx?"

"Well, you know how it is, Ray."

"Yeah, that's the truth. I know how it is."

"I was trying to impress this girl. I just met her fairly recently, and one of those cops must have recognized my name and I didn't want her to find out I've got a criminal past."

"A criminal past."

"Right."

"But that's all behind you, that criminal past. You're Stanley Straightarrow now."

"Right."

"Uh-huh." He puffed on his cigarette. I rolled down my window to let some smoke out and some New York air in, a pointless exchange if there ever was one. He said, "How do you tie in with this Sheldrake character?"

"He's my dentist."

"I got a dentist. They say to see him twice a year and that's plenty for me. I don't hang out at his office, I don't try slipping it to his nurse."

"Hygienist."

"Whatever. You a big fight fan, Bernie?"

"I get to the Garden when I can."

"This used to be a real fight town. Remember when they had a Wednesday card at St. Nick's Arena? And then you had your regular fights out at Sunnyside Gardens in Queens. You ever used to get out there?"

"I think I went two, three times. That was some years ago, wasn't it?"

"Oh, years and years," he said. "I love it that you showed Todras and Nyswander a ticket stub. Just happened to have it with you, Jesus, I really love it."

"I was wearing the same jacket."

"I know. If it was me and I was settin' up an alibi I'd have the stub in a different jacket and I'd take 'em back to my apartment and rummage through the closet until I came up with the stub. It looks better that way. Not so obvious, you know?"

"Well, I wasn't setting up an alibi, Ray. I just happened to go to the fights that night."

"Uh-huh. But if you just happened to stop there on your way home to pick up a stub that somebody else just happened to throw away, well, that would be interestin', wouldn't it? That would mean you were tryin' to set up an alibi before the general public knew there was anythin' to need an alibi for. Which might mean you knew about Sheldrake's wife gettin' bumped while the body was still warm, which would be a damned interestin' thing for you to know, wouldn't it?"

"Wonderful," I said. "The only thing worse than not having an alibi is having one."

"I know, and it's a hell of a thing, Bern. You get suspicious when you've had a few years in the Department. You lose the knack of takin' things at face value. Here all you did was take in a fight card and it looks for all the world like I'm fixin' to tag you with a felony."

"I thought it was open and shut. I thought you people figured the husband did it."

"What, the murder? Yeah, it looks as though that's how they're writin' it up. A man kills his ex-wife and leaves his own personal scalpel in her chest, that's as good as a signature, isn't it? If it was my case I might think it was a little too good, the way that ticket stub in your pocket was a little too good, but it ain't my case and what does an ordinary harness bull in a blue uniform know about something fancy like homicide? You got to wear a three-piece suit in order to be up on the finer points of these things, so I just keep my own nose clean and let the boys in suits and ties take care of the homicides. I mind my own business, Bernie."

"And what's your business exactly, Ray?"

"Now there's another good question." A light turned and he hung a right turn, his fleshy hands caressing the wheel. "I'll tell you," he said. "I think there's a reason I'm still wearin' a uniform after all these years on the force, and I think the reason's I never been a subtle guy. My trouble is I notice the obvious first and foremost. I see a ticket stub happens to be in somebody's pocket and what comes to mind is a planned alibi. And I look at the guy in question and he's a fellow that's spent his whole life liftin' things out of other people's houses, what comes to mind is a burglary. Here we got a burglar who went to some trouble settin' hisself up with an alibi, and the next mornin' we find him in the office of the dentist who just cooled out his wife, and the morning after that one he's tiptoein' out of the dentist's nurse's bedroom, and I don't know what a subtle plainclothes man would make of all that, but old Ray here, he gets right down to cases."

Ahead of us, a UPS van had traffic tied up. Some of the other drivers around us were using their horns to ventilate their feelings. But Ray was in no hurry.

I said, "I'm not sure what you're getting at."

"Well, what the hell, Bernie. Here we are, just you and me and a traffic jam, so let's us get down to carpet tacks. The way I figure it, you decided the Sheldrake dame looked like an easy score. Maybe you kept your ears open when you were gettin' your teeth drilled, or maybe you got hipped by the nurse that you been havin' a romance with, one way or another, but you decided to drop over to Gramercy and open a couple of locks and see what was loose. Now maybe you were in and out before Sheldrake came callin', but then how would you know you needed an alibi? No, I'll tell you the way I figure it. You got there and opened the door and found her with her heart stopped. You took a minute to fill your pockets with pretty things and then you got the hell out, and on the way home you stopped at the Garden and picked a stub off the floor. Then first thing the next mornin' you hopped over to Sheldrake's office to keep in touch with what was happenin' and make sure your own neck wasn't on the block."

"What makes you think something was stolen?"

"The dead woman had more jewelry than Cartier's window. There's nothin' in the apartment but prizes out of Cracker Jack boxes. I don't figure it walked away."

"Maybe she kept it in a bank vault."

"Nobody keeps it all in a bank vault."

"Maybe Sheldrake took it."

"Sure. He remembered to turn the place inside out and carry off all the jewels but he was so absent-minded that he left his whatchacallit, his scalpel, he left it in her heart. I don't think so."

"Maybe the cops took it."

"The investigatin' officers?" He clucked his tongue at me. "Bernie, I'm surprised at you. You think a couple of guys checkin' out a homicide are gonna stop to rob the dead?"

"It's been known to happen."

"Honestly? I think it's a hell of a thing. But it didn't happen this time because the downstairs neighbor was on hand when they cracked the Sheldrake woman's door. You don't steal when somebody's watchin' you. I'm surprised you didn't know that."

"Well, you don't go ahead and commit a burglary if you have to step over a corpse to get to the jewels, Ray. And I'm surprised *you* didn't know *that.*"

"Maybe."

"More than maybe."

He gave his head a dogged shake. "Nope," He said. "Maybe's as far as I'd go on that one. Because you know what you got? You got the guts of a burglar, Bernie. I remember how cool you were when me and that crud Loren Kramer walked in on you over in the East Sixties, and there's a dead body in the bedroom and you're actin' like the apartment's empty."

"That's because I didn't *know* there was a body in the bedroom. Remember?"

He shrugged. "Same difference. You got the guts of a burglar and all bets are off. Why else would you fix yourself an alibi?"

"Maybe I actually went to the fights, Ray. Ever think of that?"

"Not for very long."

"And maybe I set up an alibi—which I *didn't* because I really *was* at the fights—"

"Yeah, yeah."

"—because I was working some other job. I'm not that crazy about jewels. They're getting tougher and tougher to sell, the fences are turning vicious, you know that. Maybe I was out lifting somebody's coin collection and I established an alibi just as a matter of course, because I know you people always come knocking on my door when a coin collection walks out of its owner's house."

"I didn't hear nothin' about a coin collection stolen the other night."

"Maybe the owner was out of town. Maybe he hasn't missed it yet."

"And maybe what you robbed was a kid's piggy bank and he's too busy cryin' to tell the cops about it."

"Maybe."

"Maybe shit don't stink, Bernie. I think you got the Sheldrake woman's jewels."

86

"I don't."

"Well, you gotta say that. That don't mean I gotta believe it."

"It's the truth."

"Yeah, sure. You spent the night with Sheldrake's nurse because you didn't have no better place to stay. I believe everything you tell me, Bernie. That's why I'm still in a blue uniform."

I didn't answer him and he didn't say anything more. We drove around for awhile. The UPS truck had long since gotten out of the way and we were drifting in the stream of traffic, turning now and then, taking a leisurely ride around the streets of midtown Manhattan. If all you noticed was the weather, then you might have mistaken it for a nice fall day.

I said, "Ray?"

"Yeah, Bern?"

"There's something you want?"

"There always is. There's this book, they ran a hunk of it in the *Post. Looking Out for Number One.* Here's a whole book tellin' people to be selfish and let the other guy watch out for his own ass. Imagine anybody has to buy a book to learn what we all grew up knowin'."

"What is it you want, Ray?"

"You care for a smoke, Bernie? Oh, hell, you already told me you quit. It bother you if I smoke?"

"I can stand it."

He lit a cigarette. "Those jewels," he said. "Sheldrake's jewels that you took from her apartment."

"I didn't get them."

"Well, let's suppose you did. Okay?"

"Okay."

"Well," he said, "I never been greedy, Bern. All I want is half."

Eleven

Spyder's Parlor was dark and empty. The chairs perched on top of the tables. The stools had been inverted and set up on the bar. A menu in the window indicated that they opened for lunch during the week, but today was Saturday and they wouldn't turn the lights on until mid-afternoon. I stayed with Lexington a block or two uptown to a hole in the wall where the counterman mugged and winked and called his female patrons dear and darling and sweets. They ate it up. I ate up a sandwich, cream cheese on date-nut bread, and drank two cups of so-so coffee.

Grabow, Grabow, Grabow. In a hotel lobby I went through the Manhattan telephone directory and came up with eight Grabows plus two who spelled it without the final letter. I bought dimes from the cashier and tried all ten numbers. Six of them didn't answer. The other four didn't know anything about any artist named Grabow. One woman said her husband's brother was a painter, exteriors and interiors, but he lived upstate in Orchard Park. "It's a suburb of Buffalo," she said. "Anyway he didn't change his name, it's still Grabowski. I don't suppose that helps you."

I told her I didn't see how it could but thanked her anyway. I started to leave the hotel and then something registered in my mind and I went back to the directory and started calling Grabowskis. It would have been cute if it worked but of course it didn't, it just cost me a lot of dimes, and I called all seventeen Grabowskis and reached I don't know how many, fourteen or fifteen, and of course none of them painted anything, pictures or interiors or exteriors, none of them even colored in coloring books or painted by number, and that was the end of that particular blind alley.

The nearest bank was a block east on Third Avenue. I bought a roll of dimes—you can still get fifty of them for five dollars, it's one of the few remaining bargains—and I carried all fifty of them to another hotel lobby. I passed some outdoor phone booths on the way but they don't have phone books anymore. I don't know why. I called Spyder's Parlor to make sure it was still closed and it was. I hauled out the Yellow Pages and looked up Attorneys. See Lawyers, said the book, so I did. I don't know what I expected to find. There were eighteen pages of lawyers and plenty of them were named John, but so what? I couldn't see any reason to call any of them. I sort of flipped through the listings, hoping something would strike me, and a listing for a firm called Carson, Kidder and Diehl made me flip to the V's. I called Carson Verrill, Craig's personal attorney, and managed to get through to him. He hadn't heard anything since he'd referred Craig to Errol Blankenship and he wanted to know who I was and what I wanted. I told him I was a dentist myself and a personal friend of Craig's. I didn't bother inventing a name and he didn't press the point.

I called Errol Blankenship. He was out, I was told, and would I care to leave a name and a number?

Grabow, Grabow, Grabow. The listing for artists filled a couple of pages. No Grabow. I looked under art galleries to see if he happened to own his own gallery. If he did, he'd named it something other than Grabow.

I invested a dime and called Narrowback Gallery, on West Broadway in SoHo. A woman with a sort of scratchy voice answered the phone just when I was about to give up and try somebody else. I said, "Perhaps you'll be able to help me. I saw a painting about a month ago and I haven't been able to get it out of my mind. The thing is, I don't know anything about the artist."

"I see. Let me light a cigarette. There. Now let's see, you saw a painting here at our gallery?"

"No."

"No? Where did you see it?"

Where indeed? "At an apartment. A friend of a friend, and it turns out they bought it at the Washington Square Outdoor Art Show a year ago, or maybe it was the year before. It's all sort of vague."

"I see."

She did? Remarkable. "The only thing I know is the artist's name," I said. "Grabow."

"Grabow?"

"Grabow," I agreed, and spelled it.

"Is that a first name or a last name?"

"It's what he signed on the bottom of the canvas," I said. "For all I know it's his cat's name, but I suppose it's his last name."

"And you want to find him?"

"Right. I don't know anything about art—"

"But I'll bet you know what you like."

"Sometimes. I don't like that many paintings, but I liked this one, so much so that I can't get it out of my mind. The owners say they don't want to sell it, and then it occurred to me that I could find the artist and see what else he's done, but how would I go about it? He's not in the phone book, Grabow that is, and I don't know how to get hold of him."

"So you called us."

"Right."

"I wish you could have waited until late in the day. No, don't apologize, I should be up by now anyway. Are you just going through the book and calling every gallery you can find? Because you must own stock in the phone company."

"No, I—"

"Or maybe you're rich. Are you rich?"

"Not particularly."

" 'Cause if you're rich, or even semirich, I could show you no end of pretty pictures even if Mr. Grabow didn't paint them. Or Ms. Grabow. Why don't you come on down and see what we've got?"

"Er."

"Because we haven't got any Grabows in stock, I'm afraid. We've got a terrific selection of oils and acrylics by Denise Raphaelson. Some of her drawings as well. But you probably never heard of her."

"Well, I—"

"However, you're talking to her. Impressed?"

"Certainly."

"Really? I can't imagine why. I don't think I ever heard of a painter named Grabow. Do you have any idea how many millions of artists there are in this city? Not literally millions, but tons of 'em. Are you calling all the galleries?"

"No," I said, and when she failed to interrupt me I added, "You're the first one I called, actually."

"Honest? To what do I owe the honor?"

"I sort of liked the name. Narrowback Gallery."

"I picked it because this loft has a weird shape to it. It skinnies down as you move toward the rear. I was beginning to regret not calling it the Denise Raphaelson Gallery, what the hell, free advertising and all, but calling it Narrowback finally paid off. I got myself a phone call. What kind of stuff does Grabow paint?"

How the hell did I know? "Sort of modern," I said.

"That's a surprise. I figured he was a Sixteenth-Century Flemish master."

"Well, abstract," I said. "Sort of geometric."

"Hard-line stuff?"

What did that mean? "Right," I said.

"Jesus, that's what everybody's doing. Don't ask me why. You really like that stuff? I mean, once you get past the fact that it's interesting shapes and colors, then what have you got? As far as I'm concerned it's waiting-room art. You know what I mean by that?"

"No," I said, mystified.

"I mean you can hang it in a waiting room or a lobby and it's great, it won't offend anybody, it goes nice with the décor and it makes everybody happy, but what *is* it? I don't mean because it's not representational, I mean artistically, what the fuck is it? I mean if you want to hang it in a dentist's office that's sensational, and maybe you're a dentist and I just put my foot in my mouth. Are you a dentist?"

"Christ, no."

"You sound like you're the direct opposite of a dentist, whatever that could be. Maybe you knock people's teeth out. I'm a little flaky this morning, or is it afternoon already? Jesus, it is, isn't it?"

"Just barely."

"Gag."

"I beg your pardon?"

"That's how you can find your Grabow, though I don't think you should bother, to tell you the truth. What I think you should do is buy something beautiful by the one and only Denise Raphaelson, but failing that you can try Gag. That's initials, G-A-G, it's Gotham Artists' Guild. They're a reference service, you go there and they have slides of everybody's work in their files, plus they have everything indexed by artists' names, and they can tell you what gallery handles an artist's work or how to get in touch with him directly if he doesn't have any gallery affiliation. They're located somewhere in midtown, I think in the East Fifties. Gotham Artists' Guild."

"I think I love you."

"Honest? This is so sudden, sir. All I know about you is you're not a dentist, which is a point in your favor, truth to tell. I bet you're married."

"I bet you're wrong."

"Yeah? Living with somebody, huh?"

"Nope."

"You weigh three hundred pounds, you're four-foot-six, and you've got warts."

"Well, you're wrong about the warts."

"That's good, because they give me toads. What's your name?"

Was there any way on earth the cops were going to interrogate this lady? There was not. "Bernie," I said. "Bernie Rhodenbarr."

"God, if I married you I'd still have the same initials. I could keep on wearing all my monogrammed blouses. And yet we'll never meet. We'll have shared this magic moment over the telephone and we'll never encounter each other face to face. That's sad but it's okay. You told me you loved me and that's better than anything that happened to me all day yesterday. Gotham Artists' Guild. Got it?"

"Got it. 'Bye, Denise."

" 'Bye, Bernie. Keep in touch, lover."

. . .

Gotham Artists' Guild was located on East Fifty-fourth Street between Park and Madison. They told me over the phone to call in person, so I took a bus uptown and walked over to their office. It was two flights up over a Japanese restaurant.

I'd been winging it with Denise Raphaelson, inventing my story as I went along, but now I was prepared and I gave my spiel to an owlish young man without any hesitation. He brought me a half dozen Kodachrome slides and a viewer.

"This is the only Grabow we have," he said. "See if it looks like the painting you remember."

It didn't look anything like the painting I'd described to Denise, and I almost said as much until I remembered that the painting I'd been talking about had never existed in the first place. Grabow's work turned out to involve bold amorphous splashes of color applied according to some scheme which no doubt made considerable sense to the artist. It wasn't the kind of thing I usually liked, but I was looking at it in miniature, and maybe it would blow my mind if I saw it life-size.

As if it mattered. "Grabow," I said positively. "The painting I saw was like these, all right. It's definitely the same artist."

I couldn't get an address or a phone number. When the artist is represented by a gallery that's all they'll tell you, and Walter Ignatius Grabow was represented by the Koltnow Gallery on Green Street. That was also in SoHo, quite possibly no more than a stone's throw from Denise Raphaelson. And possibly rather more than that; my grasp of geography south of the Village is limited.

I found a pay phone—the Hotel Wedgeworth, Fifty-fifth just east of Park. I called the Koltnow Gallery and nobody answered. I called Jillian's apartment and nobody answered. I called Craig's office and nobody answered. I called 411 and asked the Information operator if there was a listing in Manhattan for Walter Ignatius Grabow. She told me there wasn't. I thanked her and she said I was welcome. I thought of calling Denise back and telling her I'd managed to get in touch with my Grabow, thanks to her good advice, but I restrained myself. I called Koltnow again, and Jillian, and Craig's office, and nothing happened. Nobody was home. I dialed my own number and established that I wasn't home either. The whole world was out to lunch.

Ray Kirschmann had staked his claim to half of Crystal's jewels and I hadn't even stolen them yet. He'd figured things wrong but he'd come scarily close to the truth. Todras and Nyswander knew the story about my aunt was a lot of crap and that I was a burglar. I had no idea if they knew there was a lot of jewelry involved in the case, and I couldn't begin to guess what they had told Jillian or what Jillian had said to them. Nor did I know anything much about Craig's situation. He was probably still in jail, and if Blankenship was any good he'd told his client to button his lip, but how many lawyers are any good? At any moment Craig might decide to start singing a song about Bernie the Burglar, and where would that leave me? I had a ticket stub between me and a homicide charge, and I couldn't make myself believe it amounted to an impregnable shield.

I walked around. It was a medium-nice fall day. The smog had dimmed the sun somewhat but it was still nice and bright out, the kind of day you don't take the trouble to appreciate until the only fresh air you get to breathe is out in the exercise yard.

Dammit, who killed the woman? W. I. Grabow? Knobby? Lawyer John? Had the murderer and the lover been one and the same? Or had the murderer killed her because he was jealous of the lover, or for an entirely different reason? And where did the jewels fit in? And where did Craig fit in? And where, dammitall, did *I* fit in?

What I kept fitting in was phone booths, and the next time I tried the Koltnow Gallery a woman answered on the second ring. She sounded older than Denise Raphaelson, and her conversation was less playful. I said I understood she represented Walter Grabow, that I was an old friend and wanted to get in touch.

"Oh, we used to have some paintings of his, though I can't remember that we ever made a sale for him. He was trying to get together enough grade-A material for a show and it never materialized. How did you know to call us?"

"Gotham Artists' Guild."

"Oh, Gag," she said. "They've still got us listed as Wally's gallery? I'm surprised. He never really caught on with anybody, you know, and then he got involved with graphics and became more interested in printmaking techniques than anything else. And he stopped painting, and I thought that was insane because his forte was his color sense, and here he was wrapping himself up in a strait jacket of detail-work. Are you an artist yourself?"

"Just an old friend."

"Then you don't want to hear all this. You just want to know where he's *at,* as the children say. Hold on a moment." I held, and after a little while the operator told me to put in another nickel. I dropped a dime in the slot and told her to keep the change. She didn't even thank me, and then the woman at Koltnow Gallery read off a number on King Street. I couldn't remember where King street was at. As the children say.

"King Street."

"Oh, I'll bet you're from out of town. Are you?"

"That's right."

"Well, King Street is in SoHo, but just barely. It's one block So of Ho." She laughed mechanically, as if she used this little play on words frequently and was getting sick of it. "South of Houston, that is."

"Oh," I said. I now remembered where King Street was, but she went on to explain just what subways I should take to get there, all that crap, none of which I needed to hear.

"This is the most recent address I have for him," she said. "I couldn't swear that he's still there, but we've kept him on our mailing list for invitations to gallery openings and the mail doesn't come back, so if you write to him the Post Office'll forward it, but—"

She went on and on. She didn't have a telephone number listed, but I could look in the phone book, unless of course I'd already done so, and maybe he had an unlisted number, and of course if I went to the King Street address and he wasn't there I could always check with the super, that was occasionally helpful, and all of this stupid advice that any fourth-grader could have figured out by himself.

The operator cut in again to ask for more money. They're never satisfied. I started to drop yet another dime in the slot, then came abruptly to my senses. And hung up.

I still had the dime in my hand. I started to put it in my pocket. Then, without any real thought involved, I began making a phone call instead. I dialed Jillian's apartment, and when a male voice answered I said, "Sorry, wrong number," and hung up. I frowned, checked the number on the card on my wallet, frowned again, fished out another dime—I still had an ample supply—and dialed once more.

"Hello?"

The same voice. A voice I'd heard often over the years, saying not *Hello* but *Open wider, please.*

Craig Sheldrake's voice.

"Hello? Anybody there?"

Nobody here but us burglars, I thought. And what are *you* doing *there?*

Twelve

King Street lies just below the southern edge of Greenwich Village, running west from Macdougal Street toward the Hudson. SoHo's a commercial district that's been turned into artists' housing, but the stretch of King where Grabow lived had always been primarily residential. Most of the block was given over to spruced-up brownstones four and five stories tall. Here and there an old commercial building newly converted to artists' lofts reminded me I was south of Houston Street.

Grabow's building was one of these. It stood a few doors off Sixth Avenue, a square structure of dull-red brick. It was four stories tall but the height of its ceilings put its roofline even with the five-story brownstones on either side. On all four floors the building sported floor-to-ceiling industrial windows extending the full width of the building, an unarguable boon to artists and exhibitionists.

A boon, too, to the veritable jungle of plants on the second floor, a tropical wall of greenery that was positively dazzling. They were soaking up the afternoon sun. The building was on the uptown side of the street so the windows faced south, which was probably terrific for the plants but less desirable for artists, who prefer a north light. On the first and third and top floors, drapes prevented the south light from screwing up masterpieces. Or perhaps the tenants were sleeping, or out for the day, or watching home movies—

I opened the door and stood in a small areaway facing another door, and this one was locked. The lock looked fairly decent. Through a window in the door—glass with steel mesh in it, they weren't kidding around here—I could see a flight of stairs, a large self-service freight elevator, and a door that presumably led into the ground-floor apartment. This last was probably a safety requirement, as the ground-floor place had its own entrance in front from the days when it had been some sort of store. The downstairs tenant got his mail through a slot in his front door, because there were only three mailboxes in the hall where I stood, each with a buzzer beneath it, and the middle box was marked Grabow. Nothing fancy, just a scrap of masking tape with the name printed in soft pencil, but it did get the message across.

So his loft figured to be the middle one of the three, which would put it two flights up. I reached for the buzzer and hesitated, wishing I had a phone number for him. After all, I had a whole pocket full of dimes. If I could call him I'd know whether or not to open his door. Hell, if I called him anything could happen. His wife could answer the phone. Craig Sheldrake could answer the phone. He was answering all sorts of phones these days—

But I didn't want to think about that. I'd cabbed downtown trying not to think at all about Craig and his surprising presence in Jillian's apartment. If I started thinking about that I'd start wondering why he was there instead of in a cell, and just when they had started letting persons charged with homicide go dancing out on bail. I might even wonder what had led the cops to drop charges against Craig, and who they were looking for to take his place.

God, why would *anyone* want to think about that?

I pushed Grabow's button. Nothing happened. I pushed it again. Nothing happened again. I gazed thoughtfully at the lock and touched the ring of cunning implements in my trouser pocket. The lock didn't scare me, but how did I know there was nobody home upstairs? Grabow was an artist. They keep odd hours in the first place, and this guy didn't have a listed phone, he might not have any phone at all, and maybe he was a temperamental bastard, and if he was sleeping or working he might just let the bell ring and say the hell with it, and then if I came bopping into his place he might be as tickled by the interruption as a hibernating bear.

"Help you?"

I hadn't even heard the door open behind me. I made myself take a breath and I turned around, arranging my face in what was supposed to be a pleasant smile. "Just looking for someone," I said.

"Who?"

"But he doesn't seem to be home, so I'll—"

"Who you looking for?"

Why hadn't I noticed either of the other tenants' names? Because I somehow knew who this man was. I had no logical reason for assuming the specter looming before me was Walter Ignatius himself, but I'd have bet all my dimes on it.

And he certainly did loom. He was immensely tall, a good six-six, and while that might make him a backcourt man in pro basketball it certainly placed him squarely in the forecourt of life. He had a broad forehead beneath a mop of straight blondish hair cut soup-bowl style. His cheekbones were prominent and the cheeks sunken. His nose had been broken once and I felt sorry for the idiot who'd done it, because Grabow looked as though he'd know how to get even.

"Uh, Mr. Grabow," I said. "I'm looking for a Mr. Grabow."

"Yeah, right. That's me."

I could see him attacking a canvas, dipping a three-inch brush in a quart can of porch paint. His hands were enormous—a little dental scalpel would have disappeared in them. If this man had wanted to kill Crystal, his bare hands would have been more lethal than any weapon they might have held.

I said, "That's odd, I expected an older man."

"I'm older'n I look. What's the problem?"

"You're Mr. William C. Grabow?"

A shake of the head. "Walter. Walter I. Grabow."

"That's odd," I said. I should have had a notebook to look in, a piece of paper, something. I got my wallet out and dug out Jillian's hair appointment card, holding it so Grabow couldn't see it. "*William C.* Grabow," I said. "Maybe they made a mistake."

He didn't say anything.

"I'm sure they made a mistake," I said, and referred again to the card. "Now you had a sister, Mr. Grabow. Is that right?"

"I got a sister. Two sisters."

"You had a sister named Clara Grabow Ullrich who lived in Worcester, Massachusetts, and—"

"No."

"I beg your pardon?"

"You got the wrong party after all. I got two sisters, Rita and Florence, Rita's a nun, Flo's out in California. What's this Clara?"

"Well, Clara Grabow Ullrich is deceased, she died several months ago, and—"

He moved a large hand, dismissing Clara Grabow Ullrich forever. "I don't have to know this," he said. "You got the wrong party. I'm Walter I. and you're looking for William."

"William C."

"Yeah, whatever."

"Well, I'm sorry to bother you, Mr. Grabow." I moved toward the door. He stepped aside to let me pass, then dropped a hand on the doorknob, just resting it there.

"Wait a minute," he said.

"Is something wrong?" Had the hulk suddenly remembered a long-lost sister? Oh, God, had he decided to try to glom onto some nonexistent legacy?

"This address," he said.

"Pardon me?"

"Where'd you get this address?"

"My firm supplied it."

"Firm? What firm?"

"Carson, Kidder and Diehl."

"What's that?"

"A law firm."

"You're a lawyer? You're not a lawyer."

"No, I'm a legal investigator. I work for lawyers."

"This address isn't listed anywhere. How'd they get it?"

"There are city directories, Mr. Grabow. Even if you don't have a phone, all tenants are—"

"I sublet this place. I'm not the tenant of record, I'm not in any directories." His head jutted forward and his eyes burned down at me.

"Gag," I said.

"Huh?"

"Gotham Artists' Guild."

"They gave you this address?"

"That's how my firm got it. I just remembered. You were listed with Gotham Artists' Guild."

"That's years back," he said, wide-eyed with wonder. "Back when I was painting. I was into color then, big canvases, I had scope, I had vision—" He broke off the reverie. "You're with this law firm," he said, "and you're coming around here on a Saturday?"

"I work my own hours, Mr. Grabow. I don't follow a nine-to-five routine."

"Is that a fact."

"Now if you'll just excuse me I'll let you go on about your business."

I made to take a step toward the door. His hand stayed on the knob.

"Mr. Grabow—"

"Who the fuck *are* you?"

God, how had I gotten myself into this mess? And how was I going to get myself out? I started running the same tape again, babbling that I was a legal investigator, repeating the name of my firm, and it was all just hanging in the air like smog. I made up a name for myself, something like John Doe but not quite that original, and then I looked at that hair appointment card again as if something on it would inspire me, and he extended a hand.

"Let's see that," he said.

It didn't have any of the information I'd been making up. All it had was Jillian's address and number on one side and some crap about an appointment with Keith on the other. And there was his great paw, beckoning.

I started to hand him the card. Then I stopped, and let out a horrible groan, and clapped my hand, card and all, to my chest.

"What in—"

"Air!" I croaked. "Air! I'm dying!"

"What the hell is—"

"My heart!"

"Look—"

"My pills!"

"Pills? I don't—"

"Air!"

He held the door open. I took a step outside, doubled over, coughing, and then I took another step, and then I straightened up and ran like a sonofabitch.

Thirteen

Happily, Walter Ignatius Grabow wasn't in the habit of spending his evenings loping around Gramercy Park. If I'd had a long-distance runner chasing after me I wouldn't have stood a chance. As it was, I don't think he even made an effort. I had a few steps on him and took him utterly by surprise, and while I didn't stop to see whether he was pounding the pavement after me, I did hear his yells of "Hey!" and "What the hell?" and "Where you going, dammit?" trailing off behind me. They trailed rather sharply, suggesting that he merely stood in place and hollered while I ran, appropriately enough, like a thief.

Unhappily, I wasn't a jogger either, and by the time I'd managed a couple of blocks on sheer adrenalin stimulated by rank cowardice, I was clutching my chest in earnest and holding onto a lamppost with my other hand. My heart was hammering in a distinctly unhealthy fashion and I couldn't catch my breath, but the old master painter was nowhere to be seen, so that meant I was safe. Two cops wanted me for murder and another cop wanted half the jewels I hadn't stolen, but at least I wasn't going to get beaten to death by a crazy artist, and that was something.

When I could breathe normally again I found my way to a bar on Spring Street. There was nothing artsy about the place or the old men in cloth caps who sat drinking shots and beers. It had been doing business long before SoHo got a face-lift, and the years had given it a cozy feel and a homey smell that was composed of equal parts of stale beer, imperfect plumbing, and wet dog. I ordered a glass of beer and spent a long time sipping it. Two gentlemen a few stools over were remembering how Bobby Thompson's home run won the 1951 pennant for the Giants. They were the New York Giants then, and as far as my fellow drinkers were concerned it all happened the day before yesterday.

"It was Ralph Branca threw that pitch. Bobby Thompson, he hit it a ton. What I always wondered is how Ralph Branca felt about it."

"Made himself immortal," the other said. "You wouldn't be remembering Ralph Branca but for that pitch he served up."

"Oh, go on."

"You wouldn't."

"Me forget Ralph Branca? Now go on."

When my beer was gone I went to the phone at the back and tried Jillian's number. While it rang I thought of things to say to Craig when he answered, but he didn't and neither did anybody else. After eight or ten rings I retrieved my dime and got Craig's home number from Information. It rang three times and he picked it up.

"Hi," I said. "I got a toothache. Let me talk to Jillian, will you?"

There was a long and thoughtful pause. Pensive, you might say. Then he said, "Sheesh, Bern, you're really cool."

"Like a burpless cucumber."

"You're something else, Bern. Where are you calling from? No, don't tell me. I don't want to know."

"You do not want de information?"

"Who are you supposed to be?"

"Peter Lorre. I know it's not very good. I do a pretty good Bogart, shweetheart, but my Peter Lorre's strictly Amateur Night. Let me talk to Jillian."

"She's not here."

"Where is she?"

"Home, I suppose. How should I know?"

"You were over there before."

"How did you—oh, you were the wrong number. Listen, Bernie, I don't think we should be having this conversation."

"You figure the line is tapped, eh, shweetheart?"

"Jesus, cut it out."

"It's not a bad Bogart impression."

"Just cut out the whole thing, will you? I've been in jail, I've been hassled by cops, my whole life's been spread all over the fucking newspapers, and my ex-wife is dead, and—"

"Well, it's an ill wind, right?"

"Huh?"

"You were praying Crystal would die, and now—"

"*Jesus!* How can you talk like that?"

"I've got the guts of a burglar. When did they let you out, anyhow?"

"Couple of hours ago."

"How did Blankenship manage that?"

"Blankenship couldn't manage the Bad News Bears. All Blankenship wanted was for me to sit tight. I kept sitting tight and I'd have gone on sitting tight while they shaved my head and attached the electrodes. Then they'd have thrown the switch and I'd have sat even tighter."

"They don't do that anymore."

"With my luck it'll come back into style. I got rid of Blankenship. The prick wouldn't believe I was innocent. How could he do me any good if he thought I was guilty?"

"My lawyer's done me loads of good over the years," I said, "and he *always* thought I was guilty."

"Well, you always were, weren't you?"

"So?"

"Well, I was innocent, Bern. I dumped Blankenship and got my own lawyer in my corner. He's not a criminal lawyer but he knows me, and he also knows his ass from a hole in the ground, and he heard me out and told me how to open up to the cops a little, and by ten o'clock this morning they were unlocking the cell door and treating me like a human being again. It made a nice change, let me tell you. Being locked up isn't my idea of a good time."

"Tell me about it. What did you give them?"

"Who?"

"The cops. Whad did you say that made them let you off the hook?"

"Nothing important. I just leveled a little, that's all."

"Leveled about what?"

Another pause, not as long as the first one. Not so much pensive this time as, well, evasive. Then, "Jillian says you've got an alibi anyway. You were at the fights."

"You bastard, Craig."

"I just told them about the jewels, that's all. And about the conversation we had."

"You told them you talked me into going after her jewels?"

"That's not what happened, Bernie." He spoke carefully, as if for the benefit of eavesdropping ears. "I was talking about Crystal's jewelry, bitching about it more or less, and you seemed very interested, and of course at the time I had no idea you were a burglar, and—"

"You're a real son of a bitch, Craig."

"You're really steamed, aren't you? Sheesh, Bern, *don't* you have an alibi? Wait a minute. *Wait. A. Minute.*"

"Craig—"

"You actually did it," he said. Maybe he believed it, maybe he was still talking to an electronic listener, maybe he was trying to rationalize blabbing my name to the law. "You went in Thursday night. She interrupted you and you panicked and stabbed her."

"You're not making much sense, Craig."

"But why would you use one of my dental scalpels? How come you just happened to have one of them in your pocket?" He was thinking his way along as he spoke and I guess he wasn't used to the process. "Wait. A. Minute! You had the whole thing planned, burglary and murder rolled into one, with me set up for it. You must have been making a pitch for Jillian, that's what it was, and you wanted me out of the way so you could have a clear field with her. *That's* what it was."

"I don't believe I'm hearing this."

"Well, you just better start believing it. Jesus, Bernie. And then you call up here and ask to speak to her. You're incredible, that's all I've got to say."

"I've got the guts of a burglar."

"You can say that again."

106

"I don't particularly want to. Craig, I—"

"I don't think we should be having this conversation."

"Oh, grow up, Craig. I want to—"

Click!

He'd hung up on me. First he handed me to the cops and now he had gone and hung up on me. I stood there holding the dead phone and shaking my head at the inhumanity of man to man. Then I fed it another dime and tried him again. It went unanswered for eight rings. I broke the connection, put the dime back in the slot, dialed again. And got a busy signal.

When Jillian's number didn't answer on a second try, I wondered if I'd gotten a couple of digits switched around. I looked through my wallet for the card she'd given me but of course I hadn't put it back after the go-round with Grabow. I checked my pockets. No luck—it was gone. She'd said the number was unlisted. I tried Information and sure enough, there was no listing for her. I dialed the number again as I remembered it and got no answer, and then I looked up and dialed the number of Craig's office and while it rang I asked myself why I was wasting my time, and before I could answer myself she picked up the phone.

She said, "Oh, thank God! I've been trying your number for hours."

"I haven't been home."

"I know. Listen, everything's going crazy. Craig's out of jail. They released him."

"I know."

"What he did, he gave them your name, told them you probably took Crystal's jewels or something like that. He sort of glossed over what he told them."

"I'll just bet he did."

"That's why those policemen came up this morning. They must have known he was going to be released and they wanted to talk to me before he did. I guess. Plus they were looking for you. I told them what you said to tell them, at least I tried to get it all right. I was nervous."

"I can imagine."

"It's good you were at the boxing matches and can prove it. I think they're trying to frame you for murder."

107

I swallowed. "Yeah," I said. "It's lucky I've got an alibi."

"Craig says they'll be looking for witnesses who saw you in Crystal's neighborhood the night she was killed. But how are they going to find anybody since you weren't there? I told him he was awful to do what he did but he said his lawyer told him it was the only way to get out of that cell."

"Carson Verrill."

"Yes, he said the other man wasn't doing him any good at all."

"Well, thank God for old Carson Verrill."

"He's not old. And I'm not very thankful for him, to tell you the truth."

"Neither am I, Jillian."

"Because I think the whole thing was really rotten all the way down the line. I mean, here you were trying to do him a favor and now look what he's done in return. I tried to tell him you were after the real killer and I don't even think he paid any attention to what I was saying. He was over at my apartment and we had a fight about it and he wound up storming out. Actually he didn't storm exactly. Actually I asked him to leave."

"I see."

"Because I think it stinks, Bernie."

"So do I, Jillian."

"And I came here because I wanted to look in the files, but so far all I've done is waste time. There's no patient anywhere in the files named Grabow."

"Well, I found Grabow. He may be a hell of a painter but he can't run worth a damn."

"If you've learned Knobby's name I'll look him up right now. I didn't happen to see anybody listed as working at Spyder's Parlor. That's the name of the place, isn't it?"

"Uh-huh."

"But I didn't look at all the cards. I also was looking for people named John and then checking to see if they were lawyers, but that's really beginning to seem hopeless."

"Forget it," I said. "That's not how this is going to get solved anyway. Look, I want to check Knobby, and there are a couple of other things I ought to see about. Where are you going to be tonight?"

"My place, I guess. Why?"

"Will you be alone?"

"As far as I know. Craig won't be coming over, if that's what you mean. Not if I have anything to say about it."

"How about if I come over?"

A pause, neither pensive nor evasive. Call it provocative. "That sounds nice," she said. "What time?"

"I don't know."

"You won't be, uh—?"

"Drunk? I'm staying away from olive oil tonight."

"I think you should stay away from Frankie while you're at it."

"Sounds like a good idea. I don't know what time I'll be over because I don't know how much time everything else is going to take. Should I call first? Yeah, I'll call first. I lost the card with your number on it. Let me get a pen. Here we go. What's your number?"

"Rhinelander seven, eighteen oh two."

"One year before the Louisiana Purchase. That's what I dialed but there was no answer. Oh, of course there wasn't, you were at the office. In fact you still are, aren't you?"

"Bernie—"

"I'm a little crazy but I'm told I have nerves of steel and that's something. It looks as though I'm going to need them, too. I'll call you."

"Bernie? Be careful."

Fourteen

"Jeez, if it ain't my old buddy," Dennis said. "Saturday night and look what a crowd fulla stiffs they get here, will ya? It's a great place during the week but on weekends everybody's home with their wife and kids. People don't have to work, they don't have to unwind after work, you know what I mean? But the parking garage business, that's no five-days-a-week operation. You run a garage and they keep you hopping around the clock, and who the hell wants to waste Saturday night on his wife and kids anyway? You're not in the garage business. You told me your line but it slipped my mind."

What had I told him? I'd said I was a burglar, but what else? "Investments," I said.

"Right. Jeez, can you believe it, I can't remember your name? I got it on the tip of my tongue."

"It's Ken. Ken Harris."

"Of course it is. Just what I was gonna say. Dennis is mine, I'm in the garage business. One thing I don't forget, though, I'll bet I remember your drink. Hey, Knobby, get your ass over here, huh? Make it another of the same for me and bring my friend Kenny here a Cutty Sark on the rocks. Am I right or am I right, Ken?"

"You're right but you're wrong, Dennis."

"How's that?"

To Knobby I said, "Just make it black coffee for the time being. I got to get sober before I go and get drunk again."

I didn't have to get sober. I'd had nothing alcoholic all day except for that solitary glass of beer on Spring Street, and a couple of hours had passed since then. But what I did have to do was stay sober because I am always sober when I work and I planned to work tonight. I was standing with my old buddy Dennis at the bar of Spyder's Parlor, and good old Knobby was building the drinks, and straight black coffee was just what the burglar ordered.

"I guess you been making the rounds, eh, Kenny?"

Who was Kenny? Oh, right. I was. "I hit a few places, Dennis."

"See Frankie anywhere?"

"No. Not tonight."

"She was supposed to drop by here after dinner. Sometimes she'll put roots down in Joan's Joynt or one of those gin mills, but she's generally pretty dependable, you know what I mean? And she's not at home. I called her a few minutes ago and nobody answered."

"She'll be around," Knobby said. His head must have earned him his name. He was young, early thirties, but his bald dome made him look older at first glance. He had a fringe of dark brown hair around a prominent and shiny head of skin. His eyebrows were thick and bushy, his jaw underslung, his nose a button and his eyes a warm liquid brown. He had a lean, wiry body and he looked good in the official Spyder's Parlor T-shirt, a bright-red affair with a design silkscreened in black, a spider's web, a leering macho spider in one corner, arms extended to welcome a hesitant girlish fly. "Ol' Frances, she's got to make her rounds," he said. "Stick around and you'll see her before the night's over."

He moved off down the bar. "She'll show or she won't," Dennis said. "Least you're here, I got a buddy to drink with. I hate to drink alone. You drink alone and you're just a boozer, know what I mean? Me, I can take the alcohol or leave it alone. I'm here for the companionship."

"I know what you mean," I said. "I guess Frankie's got things to drink about these days."

"You mean What's-her-name? That got killed?"

"Right."

"Yeah, hell of a thing. She sounded bad when I talked to her a couple hours ago."

"Depressed?"

He thought it over. "Disturbed," he said. "She was saying how they let the husband off, the veterinarian or whatever he is."

"I think he's a dentist."

"Well, same difference. She said she oughta do something. I dunno, maybe she had a few already. You know how she gets."

"Sure."

"Women don't hold it the way you and I do. It's a physical thing, Ken."

Cue or not, I acted on it, waving to Knobby and springing for a drink for Dennis and coffee for myself. When the bartender moved away I said, "Knobby here, a minute ago he called her Frances."

"Well, that's her name, Ken. Frances Ackerman."

"Everybody calls her Frankie."

"So?"

"I was, you know, just thinking." I moved my hand in a vague circle. "What's Knobby's name, you happen to know?"

"Shit, lemme think. I used to know. I *think* I used to know."

"Unless his parents named him Knobby, but what kind of name is that for a little baby?"

"Naw, they wouldn't give him a name like that. He musta had hair then. The day his mother dropped him he musta had more hair than he does today."

"Here we've bought all these drinks from him and neither of us know's the bastard's name, Dennis."

"It's funny when you put it that way, Ken." He lifted his glass, drained it. "What the hell," he said, "drink up and we'll buy another round off him and ask him who the hell he is. Or who the hell he thinks he is, right?"

It took more than one round. It took several, and I had a pretty fair case of coffee nerves building by the time we established that Knobby's first name was Thomas, that his last name was Corcoran, and that he lived nearby. On a trip to the men's room I stopped to look up Knobby in the phone book. There was a Thos Corcoran listed on East Twenty-eighth Street between First and

Second. I tried the number and let it ring an even dozen times and nobody answered. I looked over my shoulder, saw no one paying attention to me, and tore the page out of the book for future reference.

Back at the bar Dennis said, "She got a friend?"

"Huh?"

"I figured you were on the phone with a broad and I asked if she's got a friend."

"Oh. Well, she hasn't got any enemies."

"Hey, that's pretty good, Ken. I bet when he was a kid they called him Corky."

"Who?"

"Knobby. Last name's Corcoran, it figures they'll call him Corky, right?"

"I guess so."

"Shit," Dennis said. "Drink up and we'll ask the bum. Hey, Corky! Get over here, you bum!"

I put a hand on Dennis's shoulder. "I'll pass for now," I said, sliding a couple of bills across the bar for Knobby. "I've got somebody to see."

"Yeah, and she's got no enemies. Well, if she's got a friend, bring her around later, huh? I'll be here for awhile. Maybe Frankie'll drop by and have a couple, but either way I'll be holding the fort."

"So maybe I'll see you later, Dennis."

"Oh, I'll be here," he said. "Where else am I gonna go?"

Fifteen

Knobby Corcoran's building was a twelve-story prewar job with an Art Deco lobby and a doorman who thought he was St. Peter. I lurked across the street watching him make sure every supplicant was both expected and desired by a bona fide tenant. I thought of passing myself off as a tenant unknown to him, but his manner suggested this wouldn't be a breeze and I wasn't sure I had self-confidence equal to the chore.

The building on the right was a five-story brownstone. The building on the left, however, was a fourteen-story building, which, given the curiosities of superstition in the New York real-estate trade, meant it was only one story taller than Knobby's building. It too had a doorman but he hadn't been through the same assertiveness-training course as Knobby's and I could have walked past him wearing convict's stripes without creating an incident.

First, though, I had to learn the number of Knobby's apartment, and I did that by presenting myself as his visitor and watching which buzzer the doorman rang for the intercom. When no one answered I knew two things for certain—Knobby lived in 8-H and nobody was home. I walked to the far corner, came partway back, and breezed past the doorman of the building next door with a nod and a smile and a "Nice night, eh?" He agreed that it was without even looking up from his paper.

I took the elevator to the top floor and climbed a flight of stairs to the roof. Some Manhattan rooftops feature amateur astronomers and some sport courting couples and still others are given over to roof gardens. This roof, praise be to God, was empty. I walked to its edge and gazed down through the darkness for about twelve feet, which is a much greater distance to fall down than to walk across. It could have been worse—there might have been a gap between the buildings. But then I wouldn't have been there in the first place.

I must have wasted a few minutes getting my courage up. But this was nothing I hadn't done before, and if you can't contend with acrophobia when there's no way around it, well, burglary's not the right trade for you, my boy. I went over there and I jumped, and while I landed with a little pain I did so with my ankles unturned. I did a few shallow kneebends to make sure that my legs still worked, let out the breath I hadn't known I'd been holding, and made my way over to the door leading back into the building.

It was locked from the inside, but of course that was the least of my problems.

Knobby's lock was no problem, either. I got to his door just as a middle-aged man emerged from a door down the hall and began walking in my direction. I could have sworn I recognized him from one of those Haley's M-O commercials, asking his pharmacist for some commonsense advice about, uh, irregularity. I knocked on Knobby's door, frowned, said, "Yeah, it's me, man. You gonna open the door or what?"

Silence from within, of course.

"Yeah, right," I said. "But hurry it up, huh?" I looked at the approaching gentleman, caught his eye, rolled my own eyes in exasperation. "Taking a shower," I confided. "So I gotta stand here while he dries off and gets dressed and everything."

He nodded sympathetically and hurried on by, hoping no doubt that I'd keep the rest of my sorrows to myself. When he turned the corner I hauled out my ring of tools and popped Knobby's lock in less time than it takes to announce the fact. He had one of those spring locks that engages automatically when you close the door, and he hadn't bothered to use the key to engage the deadbolt, so all I had to do was snick the thing back with a strip of spring steel and give the door a push.

I slipped inside, closed the door, locked it more thoroughly than Knobby had done, and groped around for a light switch. I didn't have rubber gloves with me and this time I didn't care, because I didn't expect to steal anything. All I really wanted was to find some evidence, and once I found it I could leave it there and quick go bring it to the attention of the police. There would probably be some subtle way to do this.

If I got really lucky, of course, I might just find the caseful of jewels. In which event I would liberate my attaché case with the greater portion of its contents intact, minus a few choice and eminently tracable items which I could hide here and there on the premises where Todras and Nyswander could uncover them at their leisure. But it seemed all too probable that, if Knobby was the killer and thief, the jewels were tucked away someplace where I wouldn't find them, not left in this apartment behind an imperfectly locked door.

While I thought all of these things I was already getting busy tossing the place. This was a relatively simple job because of its size. Knobby had a studio apartment not very much bigger than Jillian's place and a good deal more sparsely furnished. There was a captain's bed in unpainted birch, a mahogany set of drawers with mismatched drawer pulls, clearly acquired secondhand, a comfortable chair and a pair of straightbacked side chairs. A stove and refrigerator and sink stood at the rear, ineffectively screened from the rest of the room by a beaded curtain.

The place was sloppy. Bartenders have to be very neat at their work and I'd spent enough hours watching them polish glasses and put things away in their proper places to assume they were just naturally precise individuals. Knobby's apartment disabused me of this notion. He had scattered dirty clothes here and there around the room, his bed was unmade, and one got the general impression that his cleaning woman had died months ago and had not yet been replaced.

I kept at it. I checked the kitchen area first. There was no cold cash in the fridge, no hot jewelry in the oven. There was, as a matter of fact, mold and dead food in the former and stale grease and crud in the latter, and I moved on to other areas as quickly as possible.

The drawers in the captain's bed contained a jumble of clothing, the wardrobe running mostly to jeans in various stages of disrepute and T-shirts, some of them red Spyder's Parlor numbers, others imprinted to promote other establishments, causes, or life styles. One drawer held a variety of contraceptive devices plus the sort of sex aids available at adult bookstores—vibrators, stimulators, and diverse rubber and leather objects the specific functions of which I could only guess at.

No jewels. No dental instruments from Celniker Dental and Optical Supply. No objects of enormous value. It had occurred to me earlier that even if Knobby had no connection with the killing, I could at least make expenses out of the visit. After all, the way things were going it looked as though I'd need money for a lawyer, or for a plane to Tierra del Fuego, or something, and when I open a door without a key I expect to get something tangible for my troubles. I'm no amateur, for God's sake. I don't do it for love.

Hopeless. He had a portable TV, a radio on the dresser top, an Instamatic camera, all items that might have gladdened the heart of a junkie who'd kicked the door in looking for the price of a bag of smack, but nothing I'd lower myself to take. There was a little cash in the top right-hand dresser drawer, accumulated tips I suppose, and I reimbursed myself for what I'd spent at the bar —and his tip was part of it, as far as that goes. Actually I did a little better than get even. There was somewhere between one and two hundred dollars in ones and fives and tens, and I scooped it all up and shook the bills down into a neat stack and found them a home on my hip. No big deal, certainly, but when I find cash around I make it mine. There was change, too, lots of it, but I left it right there and closed the drawer. You've got to have standards or where the hell are you?

Enough. I could inventory every piece of debris in the lad's apartment, but why bother? I opened his closet, I burrowed among his jackets and coats, and on the overhead shelf I saw something that made my heart turn over, or skip a beat, or stand still, or— you get the idea.

An attaché case.

Not mine. Not Ultrasuede but Naugahyde, black, shiny

Naugahyde. The Nauga and the Ultra are two altogether different animals. My disappointment at this second discovery was greater than you can possibly imagine. For one moment I'd had the jewels at hand and the murder of Crystal Sheldrake all solved, and now that moment was over and I was back where I'd started.

Naturally I took the case down and opened it anyway.

Naturally I was somewhat surprised to find it absolutely jam-packed with money.

Sixteen

The bills were arranged in inch-thick stacks with buff-colored paper bands around their middles. The stacks rested on their edges so that I couldn't tell whether the bills were singles or hundreds. For a moment I just stared and wondered. Then I dug out one of the little stacks and riffled through it. The bills were twenties, and I had perhaps fifty of them in my hand. Say a thousand dollars in that stack alone.

I sampled a few other stacks. They also consisted of twenty-dollar bills, all fresh and crisp. I was looking at—what? A hundred thousand dollars? A quarter of a million?

Ransom money? A drug payoff? Transactions of that sort usually called for old bills. An under-the-table stock deal? A real-estate transaction, all cash and off the books?

And how did any of these notions mesh with Knobby Corcoran, a bartender who lived in one disorderly room, owned hardly any furniture, and couldn't be bothered to double-lock his door?

I gave the money itself some further study. Then I took ten fresh twenties from the stack and added them to the bills in my wallet. I tucked the rest back in place, closed the case, fastened the hasps.

I put his tip money back. I'd incorporated his funds with my own and hadn't kept a close count on what I'd taken, but I didn't figure he knew, either. I returned around a hundred dollars in assorted bills to his top left-hand dresser drawer, thought about it, and added one of the twenties to the collection. I dropped another bill behind the drawer so that it could only be found by someone who was searching for it. I placed a third bill out of sight at the rear of the closet shelf and wedged a fourth into one of a pair of worn cowboy boots that stood at the back of the closet.

Neat.

I turned out the light, let myself out, closed the door behind me. The elevator took me down to the lobby and the doorman wished me good evening. I gave him a curt nod; the soles of my feet still ached from that jump and I blamed him for it.

A cab came along the minute I got to the street. Sometimes things just work out that way.

They have these lockers all over New York, in subway stations, at railroad terminals. I used one at Port Authority Bus Terminal on Eighth Avenue; I opened the door, popped the attaché case inside, dropped a pair of quarters in the slot, closed the door, turned the key, took the key out and carried it off with me. It had felt very odd, carrying all that currency around with me, and it felt even odder abandoning it like that in a public place.

But it would have been stranger still running down to SoHo with it.

God knows I didn't want to go there. It hadn't been that long since I'd faked a heart attack to get away from Walter Ignatius Grabow, and here I was climbing right back onto the horse and sticking my head in the lion's mouth again.

But I told myself it wasn't all that dangerous. If he was home he'd buzz back when I rang his bell, and I'd just make an abrupt U-turn and take off. And he wouldn't be home anyway, because it was Saturday night and he was an artist and they all go out and drink on Saturday night. He'd be partying it up at somebody else's loft or knocking back boilermakers at the Broome Street Bar or sharing a jug of California Zinfandel with someone of the feminine persuasion.

Except that his girl friend Crystal was dead, and maybe he'd be doing some solitary drinking to her memory, sitting in the dark in his loft, downing shots of cheap rye and not answering the bell when I rang, just moping in a corner until I popped his lock and sashayed flylike into his parlor—

Unpleasant thought.

The thought stayed with me after I rang his bell and got no answer. The lock on the downstairs door was a damned good one and the metal stripping where the door met the jamb kept me from prying the bolt back, but no lock is ever quite so good as the manufacturer would have you believe. I did a little of this and a little of that and the pins dropped and the tumblers tumbled.

I walked up two flights. The second-floor tenant, the one with all the plants, had soft rock playing on the stereo and enough guests to underlay the music with a steady murmur of conversation. As I passed his door I smelled the penetrating aroma of marijuana, its smoke an accompaniment to the music and the talk. I went up another flight and listened carefully at Grabow's door, but all I could hear was the music from the apartment below. I got down on hands and knees and saw that no light was visible beneath his door. Maybe he was downstairs, I thought, getting happily stoned and tapping his foot to the Eagles and telling everybody about the lunatic he'd cornered that afternoon in the lobby.

Meanwhile, the lunatic braced himself and opened the door. Grabow had a good thick slab of a door, and holding it in place was a Fox police lock, the kind that features a massive steel bar angled against the door and mounted in a plate bolted to the floor. You can't kick a door in when it has that kind of a lock, nor can you take a crowbar and pry it open. It's about the strongest protection there is.

Alas, no lock is stronger than its cylinder. Grabow's had a relatively common five-pin Rabson, mounted with a flange to discourage burglars from digging it out. Why should I dig it out? I probed it with picks and talked to it with my fingers, and while it played the maiden I played Don Juan, and who do you think won that round?

Grabow lived and worked in one enormous room, with oceans of absolutely empty space serving to divide the various areas of bedroom and kitchen and living room and work space from one another. The living-room area consisted of a dozen modular sofa units covered in a rich brown plush and a couple of low parson's tables in white Formica. The sleeping area held a king-size platform bed with a sheepskin throw on it. Individual sheepskin rugs covered the floor around the bed. The wall behind the bed was exposed brick painted a creamy buff a little richer than the paper wrapper on the twenty-dollar bills, and hanging on that wall were a shield, a pair of crossed spears, and several primitive masks. The pieces looked to be Oceanic, New Guinea or New Ireland, and I wouldn't have minded having them on my own wall. Nor would I have minded having what they'd be likely to bring at a Parke-Bernet auction.

The kitchen was a beauty—large stove, a fridge with an automatic ice-maker in the door, a separate freezer, a double stainless-steel sink, a dishwasher, a washer-drier. Copper and stainless-steel cookware hung from wrought-iron racks overhead.

The work area was just as good. Two long narrow tables, one chest height, the other standard. A couple of chairs and stools. Printmaking equipment. A ceramicist's kiln. Floor-to-ceiling steel shelving filled with neatly arranged rows of paints and chemicals and tools and gadgets. A hand-cranked printing press. A few boxes of 100 percent rag-content bond paper.

It must have been around 10:15 when I opened his door, and I suppose I spent twenty minutes giving the apartment a general search.

Here are some of the things I did not find: A human being, living or dead. An attaché case, Ultrasuede or Naugahyde or otherwise. Any jewelry beyond some mismatched cufflinks and a couple of tie clips. Any money beyond a handful of change which I found —and left—on a bedside table. Any paintings by Grabow or anyone else. Any artwork except for the Oceanic pieces over the bed.

Here's what I did find: Two pieces of meticulously engraved copper plate, roughly two and a half by six inches, mounted on blocks of three-quarter-inch pine. A key of the type likely to fit a safe-deposit box. A desktop pencil holder, covered in richly embossed red leather, containing not pencils but various implements of the finest surgical steel, each fitted with a hexagonal handle.

When I left Walter Grabow's loft I took nothing with me that had not been on my person when I came. I did move one or two of his possessions from their accustomed places to other parts of the loft, and I did place several crisp new twenty-dollar bills here and there.

But I didn't steal anything. There was a moment, I'll admit, when I had the urge to fit one of those masks over my face, snatch the shield and a spear from the wall, and race through the streets of SoHo emitting wild Oceanic war whoops. The impulse was easily mastered, and I left masks and spears and shield where they hung. They were nice, and undeniably valuable, but when you've just stolen somewhere in the neighborhood of a quarter of a mill in cash, lesser larceny does seem anticlimatic.

Just as my cab pulled up in front of Jillian's building I spotted the blue-and-white cruiser next to the hydrant. "Keep going," I said. "I'll take the corner."

"I already threw the flag," my driver complained. "I'm risking a ticket."

"What's life without taking chances?"

"Yeah, you can say that, friend. You're not the one who's taking 'em."

Indeed. His tip was not all it might have been and I watched him drive off grumbling. I walked back to Jillian's, staying close to the buildings and keeping an eye open for other police vehicles, marked or unmarked. I didn't see any, nor did I notice any coplike creatures lurking in the shadows. I lurked in the shadows myself, and after a ten-minute lurk a pair of familiar shapes emerged from Jillian's doorway. They were Todras and Nyswander, not too surprisingly, and it was nice to see them still on the job after so many hours. I was happy to note that their schedule was as arduous as my own.

When they drove off I stayed right where I was for five full minutes in case they were going to be cute and circle the block. When this didn't happen I considered calling from the booth on the corner to make sure the coast was clear. I didn't feel like bothering. I buzzed Jillian from the vestibule.

All the distortion of the intercom couldn't hide the anxiety in her voice. She said, "Yes? Who is it?"

"Bernie."

"Oh. I don't—"

"Are you alone, Jillian?"

"The police were just here."

"I know. I waited until they left."

"They say you killed Crystal. They say you're dangerous. You never went to the boxing matches. You were in her apartment, you killed her—"

All this over the intercom, yet. "Can I come up, Jillian?"

"I don't know."

I'll pick the fucking lock, I thought, *and I'll huff and I'll puff and I'll kick your door in.* But I said, "I've made a lot of progress tonight, Jillian. I know who killed her. Let me up and I'll explain the whole business."

She didn't say anything, and for a moment I wondered if she'd heard me. Perhaps she had closed the intercom switch. Perhaps at this very moment she was dialing 911, and in a scant hour the swift and efficient New York police would arrive with drawn guns. Perhaps—

The buzzer buzzed and I opened the door.

She wore a wool skirt, a plaid of muted greens and blues, and a navy sweater. Her tights were also navy, and on her little feet she wore deerskin slippers with pointed toes that suited her elfin quality. She poured me a cup of coffee and apologized for giving me a hard time over the intercom.

"I'm a nervous wreck tonight," she said. "I've had a parade of visitors tonight."

"The cops?"

"They came at the very end. Well, you know that, you saw them leave. First there was another policeman. He told me his name—"

"Ray Kirschmann?"

"That's right. He said he wanted me to give you a message. I said I wouldn't be hearing from you but he gave me a very knowing wink. I wouldn't be surprised if I blushed. It was that kind of a wink."

"He's that kind of a cop. What was the message?"

"You're supposed to get in touch with him. He said you've really got the guts of a burglar and you proved it going back to the scene of the crime. He said something about he's sure you got what you went there for and he'll want to be on hand to check it out. When I told him I didn't really understand he said you would understand, and that the main thing was that you should get in touch with him."

" 'Back to the scene of the crime.' What's that supposed to mean?"

"I think I know from something the other cops said. And other things. After Kirschmann left Craig came over."

"I thought you told him not to."

"I did, but he came anyway and it was easier to let him come up than make a fuss. I told him he couldn't stay."

"What did he want?"

She made a face. "He was horrid. He really thinks you killed Crystal. He said the police were sure of it and he blames himself for setting it up for you to steal the jewels. That was what he really wanted to tell me—to deny that you had any arrangement with him. He said you'd probably blab if the police arrested you and that it would be his word against yours and naturally they'd take the word of a respectable dentist over that of a convicted burglar—"

"Naturally."

"—but that I would have to swear that your story was a lot of nonsense or he might be in trouble. I said I didn't believe you would kill anybody and he got very mad and accused me of siding with you against him, and I got nasty myself, and I don't know what I ever saw in him, I swear I don't."

"He's got nice teeth."

"Then when he left, I was just getting interested in television when his lawyer came over."

"Verrill?"

"Uh-huh. I think he came over mainly to back up Craig. Craig told him about the arrangement with you and naturally he wouldn't want that to come out, and he tried to let me know how important it was to keep it a secret. I think he was building up to offer me a bribe but he didn't come right out and say it."

"Interesting."

"He was really pretty slick, but in a very Establishment way. As if the kind of bribe I could expect wouldn't be an envelope full of cash but some sort of tax-free trust fund. Not really, but he had that kind of attitude. He said there was no question you murdered Crystal. He said the police had evidence."

"What kind of evidence?"

"He didn't say." She looked away, swallowed. "You didn't kill her, did you, Bernie?"

"Of course not."

"But you'd say that anyway, wouldn't you?"

"I don't know what I'd say if I killed her. I've never killed anybody so the question's never come up. Jillian, why on earth would I kill the woman? If she came in and caught me in the act, all I'd want to do would be to get away before the police came. Maybe I'd give her a shove to get out of there, if I had to—"

"Is that what happened?"

"No, because she didn't catch me. But if she did, and if I did shove her, and if she took a bad fall, well, I can see how a person could get hurt that way. It's never happened yet but I suppose it's possible. What's not possible is that I'd stab her in the heart with a dental scalpel I wouldn't have with me in the first place."

"That's what I told myself."

"Well, you were right."

Her eyes widened, her lower lip trembled. She gnawed prettily at it. "Those two policemen got here about three-quarters of an hour after Mr. Verrill left. They said you broke into Crystal's apartment again last night. There were police seals on it and it was broken into. They say you did it."

"Somebody hit Crystal's place again?" I frowned, trying to figure it. "Why would I do that?"

"They said you must have left something behind. Or you wanted to destroy evidence."

That was what Kirschmann has been talking about. He thought I'd make a second trip for the jewels. "Anyway," I said, "I was here last night."

"You could have stopped on the way here."

"I couldn't have stopped anywhere last night. I couldn't see straight, if you'll remember."

She avoided my eyes. "And the night before that," she said. "They say they have a witness who spotted you leaving Crystal's building right around the time she was killed. And they have another woman who says she actually spoke to you in Gramercy Park earlier that night."

"Shit. Henrietta Tyler."

"What?"

126

"A sweet little old lady who hates dogs and strangers. I'm surprised she remembered me. And that she talked to the law. I figured no one who hates dogs and strangers can be all bad. What's the matter?"

"Then you were there!"

"I didn't kill anybody, Jillian. Burglary was the only felony I committed that night, and I was busy committing it while somebody else killed Crystal."

"You were—"

"On the premises. In the apartment."

"Then you saw—"

"I saw the closet door from the inside, that's what I saw."

"I don't understand."

"I don't blame you. I didn't *see* who killed her but I had a busy night tonight and now I *know* who killed her. It all fits, even the second break-in." I leaned forward. "Do you suppose you could put up a fresh pot of coffee? Because it's a long story."

Seventeen

She listened with appropriately wide eyes while I re-created the circumstances of the burglary and the murder. When I moved along to the story of my visit to Knobby Corcoran's humble digs, she stared in awe and admiration. I may have improved on reality a bit, come to think of it. I may have made the drop from one rooftop to the other greater than it actually was, and I may have added a gap of a few yards between the buildings. Poetic license, you understand.

When I got to the attaché case she made oohing sounds. When it was Naugahyde instead of Ultrasuede she groaned, and when I opened it up and found all that money she gasped. "So much money," she said. "Where is it? You don't have it with you, do you?"

"It's in a safe place. Or else I wasted fifty cents."

"Huh?"

"Nothing important. I stashed the attaché case but I held onto a few bills because I thought they might come in handy." I took out my wallet. "I've got two left. See?"

"What about them?"

"Nice, aren't they?"

"They're twenty-dollar bills. What's so special about them?"

"Well, if you saw a whole suitcase full of them you'd be impressed, wouldn't you?"

"I suppose, but—"

"Compare the serial numbers, Jillian."

"What about them? They're in sequence. Wait a minute, they're not in sequence, are they?"

"Nope."

"They're . . . Bernie, both of these bills have the same serial number."

"Really? Jesus, that's remarkable, isn't it?"

"Bernie—"

"A world where no two snowflakes are the same, where every human being has a different set of fingerprints, and here I go and take two twenties out of my wallet and I'll be damned if they don't both have the same serial number. It makes you think, doesn't it?"

"Are they—?"

"Phony? Yeah, that's what it means, I'm afraid. Hell of a note, isn't it? All that money and all it is is green paper. Take a close look, Jillian, and you'll see it's a long way from perfect. The portrait of Andy Jackson is damn good compared to most counterfeits I've seen, but if you really look at the bill it doesn't look wonderful."

"Around the seal here—"

"Yeah, the points aren't sharp. And if you turn the bill over you'll see some other faults. Of course these bills are new ones. If you age them and distress them a little, give 'em fold lines and take the newness out of the paper by cooking them with a little coffee —well, there are tricks in every trade and I don't pretend to know some of the ones counterfeiters have come up with lately. I have enough work staying ahead of the locksmiths. I'll tell you, though, those bills you've got in your hand would pass banks nineteen times out of twenty. The serial number's about the only obvious fault. Would you look twice at one of these if you got it in change?"

"No."

"Neither would anybody else. As soon as I saw the money was counterfeit I went straight back to Grabow's place. One step inside the door and I knew I was on the right track. He was an unsuccessful artist who'd turned to printmaking and had made no big success of that, and here he was living in a loft most New Yorkers would kill for, tons of space, beautiful furniture, a few thousand dollars' worth of primitive artifacts on the wall. I poked around and found enough inks and paper to make better money than the Bureau of Engraving and Printing turns out, and if there was any doubt it vanished when I found the actual printing plates. He does beautiful line work. It's really high-quality engraving."

"Grabow's a counterfeiter?"

"Uh-huh. I wondered why he was so suspicious when he had me trapped in the vestibule of his building. I did a pretty good job of looking like a dumb schmuck who was chasing the wrong Grabow, but he was full of questions. Who was I? How'd I get his address? How come I was working on a Saturday? He came up with questions faster than I could come up with answers, that's why I had to run out on him, but why would he have so many suspicions if he didn't have something to hide? Yes, he's a counterfeiter. I can't swear that he made the plates himself, but he's got them now. And he certainly did the printing."

"And then he gave the money to Knobby Corcoran? I don't understand what happened next."

"Neither do I, but I can make a few guesses. Suppose Crystal brought Knobby and Grabow together. Grabow was her boyfriend and maybe she took him around the bars a few times. That's what she did with the Legal Beagle, her other boyfriend, so why wouldn't she do the same thing with Grabow?

"Anyway, Grabow and Corcoran set something up. Maybe Grabow was going to produce the counterfeit twenties and Knobby was going to find a way to turn them into real money. There was some kind of a doublecross. Say Knobby wound up with the twenties and Grabow wound up talking to himself. Maybe Crystal crossed him one way or another, maybe *she* wound up with the money."

"How?"

I shrugged. "Beats me, but it could have happened. Or maybe the deal with the counterfeit went fine but Grabow found out she was just using him, two-timing him with other men and stringing him along for the sake of the counterfeiting deal. Maybe he learned she was sleeping with Knobby, maybe he found out about the other boyfriend. He got jealous and he got mad and he picked up a dental scalpel and went after her."

"Where would he get a dental scalpel?"

"Celniker Dental and Optical, same as Craig."

"But why would he—"

"He's got a whole collection of them. All sorts of picks and probes and scalpels, and it looks to me as though they're all made by Celniker unless other manufacturers also put hexagonal shafts on their instruments. I suppose they're handy for printing and printmaking, cutting linoleum blocks, making woodcuts, any of that sort of detail work. Either he took one along as a murder weapon or he just happened to have one in his pocket."

"That seems strange, doesn't it?"

It did at that. "Try it this way, then. He'd had Crystal up to his loft and she spotted the tools and mentioned that Craig had the same kind at his office. After all, she was his hygienist back before she married him. Matter of fact, that could explain the coincidence of Grabow having the same kind of tools as Craig. Maybe he was using something else, X-acto knives or God knows what, and Crystal told him he should get a set of dental instruments because the steel's high quality or whatever the hell she told him. Anyway, if he knew Craig used Celniker instruments, he could have taken the scalpel along to make it look as though Craig did the killing. He wouldn't have any reason to get rid of his own Celniker tools because there's nothing to connect him with Crystal in the first place, and once Craig's tagged with the crime the cops won't have any reason to look any further."

"So he took the scalpel along with the intention of using it as a murder weapon?"

"He must have."

"And he picked her up and went to bed with her first?"

"That would have been fiendish, wouldn't it? I just met him briefly but I didn't get the impression that he was that devious a person. He struck me as pretty direct, the strong and silent type. When she went out to the bar she probably met the Legal Beagle and brought him back. I don't remember their conversation very well because I was making such a determined effort to ignore it, but it certainly wasn't Grabow. At least I don't think it was.

"No, here's what I figure happened. Say Grabow was watching the house, or maybe he tracked her from the bar where she met the lawyer. Or whoever she met, it doesn't have to be the lawyer.

In fact we can forget about the lawyer because I don't think he really enters into it. The fact that Frankie Ackerman mentioned three men as friends of Crystal's doesn't mean all three of them are involved in her murder. It's remarkable enough that two of them are."

"Anyway," Jillian prompted, "she brought home some man or other and Grabow was watching."

"Right. Then the guy left. Grabow saw him leave. He gave him a minute or two to get lost, then came on over and leaned on the bell. When Crystal let him in, he did his strong and silent number and stuck the scalpel straight into her heart."

Jillian clutched her own heart, her small hand pressing high on the left-hand side of the navy sweater. She was following the line as if it were a movie and she were seeing it on TV.

"Then he came on into the bedroom," I went on. "First thing he saw was my attaché case standing against the wall under the French woman's portrait. He went over and—"

"What French woman?"

"It's not important. A picture on Crystal's wall. But he didn't see the picture because he only had eyes for the attaché case. See, he figured an attaché case is an attaché case. He assumed it was full of the counterfeit money and this was his chance to swipe it back."

"But the money was in a black vinyl case, wasn't it?"

"Black Naugahyde. Right. But how would Grabow know that?"

"Wouldn't he have packed it like that to begin with?"

"Maybe, but how do we know that? Maybe he gave Crystal the money in a Bloomingdale's shopping bag. That's what I usually use on burglaries. It looks like you belong, striding along with a Bloomie's bag full of someone else's property. Suppose he just knew someone had transferred it to an attaché case, and here was an attaché case, the very item he was looking for. The natural thing would be for him to grab it and get the hell out and worry later what was in it."

"And later, when he opened the case—"

"It probably confused the daylights out of him. For a minute he must have thought Crystal was some kind of medieval alchemist who managed to transmute paper into gold and diamonds. Then when he had it figured he had to go back for the money. That would explain the second break-in, the burglary after the police had already sealed the apartment. Grabow went back for the money, broke the seals, searched the place, and went home empty-handed. Because the counterfeit bills were all packed up at Knobby Corcoran's apartment, sitting on a shelf in the closet."

Jillian nodded, then frowned. "What happened to the jewels?"

"I suppose Grabow held onto them. People tend to retain jewelry rather than leave it for the garbage man. I didn't see them around his loft, but that doesn't necessarily mean anything. The jewels are evidence and he wouldn't leave them lying around because they'd lock him into the murder."

"He kept the dental tools around."

"That's different. There's no way to explain the jewelry and he'd have to realize that. He must have stashed it somewhere. It's possible he tucked it away right there on King Street. It wouldn't be terribly difficult to hide the jewels under the floorboards or inside the modular furniture where I wouldn't find them on a routine search. As far as that goes, I found a safe-deposit key among his other stuff. It's possible the jewels are already in the bank. He could have gone Friday before the banks closed and stashed them in his safe-deposit box. Or he might even have fenced them. That's not inconceivable. As a counterfeiter, the odds are he knows somebody who knows somebody who fences stolen gems. It's no harder to find a fence in this town than it is to place a football bet or buy a number or score drugs. But there's really no reason to speculate about the jewels. There's already enough evidence against Grabow to put him away for years."

"You mean the dental tools?"

"That's a start," I said. "I moved things around at his place, just in case he decides to get rid of the evidence. I put some of the twenties where you'd have to search to find them. Same with a few dental instruments. If he panics and throws out the instruments, there'll be a few he won't find that the police would turn up easily on a search. And I hid the printing plates. That might make him panic if he goes looking for them, but the way I left things he'll never believe a burglar set foot in the place. I even picked the lock on my way out to relock it, and that's a service relatively few burglars perform for you. I left his loft empty-handed, you know.

In fact I walked out of there with less than I brought, since I planted those fake twenties on him. If I did that all the time I'd have a problem coming up with the rent every month."

She giggled. "My mother used to say that if burglars came to our house they'd leave something. But you're the only one I ever heard of who actually did."

"Well, I'm not going to make a habit of it."

"Have you been a burglar all your life, Bernie?"

"Well, not all my life. I started out as a little kid, just like everybody else. I love the way you giggle, incidentally. It's very becoming. I guess I've been a burglar ever since I got done being a kid."

"I don't think you ever did get done being a kid, Bernie."

"I sometimes have that feeling myself, Jillian."

And I got to talking about myself and my crazy criminous career, how I'd started out sneaking into other people's houses for the sheer thrill of it and learned before long that the thrill was all the keener if you stole something while you were at it. I talked and she listened, and somewhere in the course of things we finished the coffee and she broke out a perfectly respectable bottle of Soave. We drank the chilled white wine out of stemmed glasses and sat side-by-side on the couch, and I went on talking and wished the couch would do its trick of converting into a bed. She was lovely, Jillian was, and she was a most attentive listener, and her hair smelled of early spring flowers.

Around the time the bottle became empty she said, "What are you going to do now, Bernie? Now that you know who the killer is."

"Find a way to get that information to the cops. I suppose I'll run the play through Ray Kirschmann. It's not his case but he smells money and that'll make him bend procedures like pretzels. I don't know how he's going to make a dollar out of this one. If the jewels turn up they'll be impounded as evidence. But if there's a buck in it he'll find it, and that'll be his problem and not mine."

"I know he wants you to call him."

"Uh-huh. But not now, I'm afraid. It's the middle of the night."

"What time is it? Oh, it really *is* the middle of the night. I didn't realize it was so late."

134

"I'll have to find someplace to stay. I'm afraid my own apartment's no good for the time being. They probably don't have it staked out but I'm not going to risk it now, not if they've got a pick-up order out on me. I can get a hotel room."

"Don't be ridiculous."

"You figure that might be dangerous? I suppose you're right. Hotels don't get that many check-ins at this hour and it might look suspicious. Well, there's something else I could always try. Just scout an empty apartment, one where the tenants are gone for the weekend, and make myself right at home. That worked well enough for Goldilocks."

"Don't be ridiculous. You stayed here last night and you can stay here again. I don't want you to take a chance of getting arrested."

"Well, Craig might—"

"Don't be ridiculous. Craig won't be coming over and I wouldn't let him in if he did. I'm pretty angry with Craig, if you want to know. I think he behaved terribly and he may be a great dentist but I'm not sure he's a very wonderful human being."

"Well, that's great of you," I said. "But this time I'll take the chair."

"Don't be ridiculous."

"Well, you're not going to sit up in that thing, for God's sake. I'm not going to let you give up your bed again."

"Don't be ridiculous."

"Huh? I don't—"

"Bernie?" She gazed up at me from beneath those long eyelashes. "Bernie, don't be ridiculous."

"Oh," I said, and looked deeply into her eyes, and smelled her hair. "*Oh.*"

Eighteen

It must have been around ten when we woke up the next morning. There were a few churches on the block and it kept being some denomination's turn to ring bells. We lay in bed for the next two hours, sometimes listening to the church bells and sometimes ignoring them. There are worse ways to spend a Sunday morning.

Finally she got up and put on a robe and made coffee while I set about getting into the same clothes I seemed to have been wearing forever. Then I got on the phone.

Ray Kirschmann's wife said he was out. Working, she said. Did I want to leave a message? I didn't.

I tried him at the precinct. He had the day off, somebody told me. Probably at home with his feet up and a cold beer in his fist and a ball game on television. Was there anybody else I would talk to? There wasn't. Did I want to leave a message? I didn't.

Did I dare go home? I wanted a shower but there wasn't much point taking one if I had to put on the same clothes again. And it was Sunday, so I couldn't go out and buy a shirt and socks and underwear.

I picked up the phone again and dialed my own number.

The line was busy.

Well, that doesn't necessarily prove anything. Somebody else could have called me a few seconds before I did; he'd get an unanswered ring while I got a busy signal. So I hung up and gave him a minute to get tired of the game, and then I dialed my number again, and it was still busy.

Well, that didn't prove anything either. Perhaps I'd had a visitor who knocked the phone off the hook. Perhaps phone lines were down on the West Side. Perhaps—

"Bernie? Something wrong?"

"Yes," I said. "Where's the phone book?"

I looked up Mrs. Hesch and dialed her number. When she answered I heard her television set in the background, then her dry cigarette-hardened voice. I said, "Mrs. Hesch, this is Bernard Rhodenbarr. Your neighbor? Across the hall?"

"The burglar."

"Uh, yes. Mrs. Hesch—"

"Also the celebrity. I seen you on television maybe an hour ago. Not you personally, just a picture they had of you. It must have been from prison, your hair was so short."

I knew the picture she meant.

"Now we got cops all over the building. They was here asking about you. Do I know you're a burglar? they asked me. I said all I know is you're a good neighbor. I should tell them anything? You're a nice young man, clean cut, you dress decent, that's all I know. You work hard, right? You make a living, right?"

"Right."

"Not a bum on welfare. If you take from those rich momsers on the East Side, do I care? Did they ever do anything for me? You're a good neighbor. You don't rob from this building, am I right?"

"Right."

"But now there's cops in your apartment, cops in the halls. Taking pictures, ringing doorbells, this, that and the other thing."

"Mrs. Hesch, the cops. Was there—"

"Just a minute, I got to light a cigarette. There."

"Was there a cop named Kirschmann?"

"Cherry."

"Jerry?"

"No, Cherry. That's Kirsch in German. Kirschmann he told me, Cherry Man is what went through my mind. He could lose thirty pounds and he wouldn't miss it."

"He's there?"

"First two of them came to my door, a million questions they had for me, and then this Kirschmann came with the same questions and a hundred others. Mr. Rhodenbarr, you ain't a killer, are you?"

"Of course not."

"That's what I told them and what I said to myself, that's what I always said about you. You didn't kill that *nafkeh* by Gramercy Park?"

"No, of course not."

"Good. And you didn't—"

"What did you call her?"

"A *nafkeh.*"

"What does that mean?"

"A whore, you should pardon the expression. You didn't kill the man either, did you?"

What man? "No, of course not," I said. "Mrs. Hesch, could you do me a favor? Could you get Ray Kirschmann to come to the phone without letting anybody know that's what you want? You could say you have something you just remembered about me, find some way to get him into your apartment without letting the other policemen know what's happening."

She could and did. It didn't take her very long, either, and all at once I heard a familiar voice, careful, cagey, say, "Yeah?"

"Ray?"

"No names."

"No names?"

"Where the hell are you?"

"On the phone."

"You better tell me where. You and me, we better get together right away. You really stepped in it this time, Bernie."

"I thought you said no names."

"Forget what I said. You were pretty cute, hitting the dame's apartment a second time and coming up with the loot. But you shoulda connected with me right away, Bern. I don't know what I can do for you now."

"You can lock up a killer, Ray."

"That's what I can do, all right, but I never figured you for a killer, Bern. It's a surprise to me."

"It would be a bigger surprise to me, Ray. As far as the jewels are concerned—"

"Yeah, well, we found 'em, Bern."

"What?"

"Right where you left 'em. If it was just me it's a different story, but I had to break my ass to get here along with Todras and Nyswander, let alone gettin' here ahead of 'em, and it was Nyswander who found the stuff. A diamond bracelet and an emerald doodad and those pearls. Beautiful."

"Just three pieces?"

"Yeah." A pause, speculative in nature. "There was more? You got the rest stashed somewhere else, right, Bern?"

"Somebody planted those pieces, Ray."

"Sure. Somebody's givin' away jewelry. Christmas is comin' up in a few months and somebody's got the spirit ahead of schedule."

I took a deep breath and plunged ahead. "Ray, I never stole the jewels. They were planted on me. The man who stole them is the same man who killed Crystal, and he planted a handful of the jewels in my apartment, at least I guess that's where you found them—"

"I didn't find 'em. Nyswander found 'em and that tears it because the bastard's incorruptible. And you bet your ass they were in your apartment, Bern, 'cause that's where you left 'em."

I let it pass. "The man who did it, the theft and the murders, is somebody you probably never heard of."

"Try me."

"He's dangerous, Ray. He's a killer."

"You were gonna tell me his name."

"Grabow."

"Somebody I never heard of, you said."

"Walter I. Grabow. The I stands for Ignatius, if that matters. I don't suppose it does."

"Funny."

"It's complicated, Ray. The plot's pretty involved. I think we ought to meet somewhere, the two of us, and I could explain it to you."

"I just bet you could."

"Huh?"

"We better meet somewhere, that's the truth. Bernie, you know what happened to you? Somewhere along the line you went bananas. I think it was the second murder that unhinged you."

"What are you talking about?"

"I never figured you for a killer," he went on. "But I suppose you could do it, as cool as you are. The second killing, in your apartment and all, I guess it unhinged you."

"*What are you talking about?*"

"Sayin' I never heard of him. Grabow, for Christ's sake. Sayin' he's dangerous. Here's the poor sonofabitch lyin' dead on the floor of your apartment with one of them dentist things in his heart and you're tellin' me he's dangerous. Jesus, Bern. You're the one who's dangerous. Now how about if you tell me where you are and I'll bring you in nice and safe so you don't get shot by somebody who's gun-happy? It's the best way, believe me. You get yourself a good lawyer and you're on the street in seven years, maybe twelve or fifteen at the outside. Is that so bad?"

He was still talking, earnest, sincere, when I cradled the receiver.

Nineteen

"I've got him on the run now," I said to Jillian. "He's starting to panic. He knows I'm closing in on him and he's scared."

"Who, Bernie?"

"Well, that's a good question. If I knew who he was I'd be in a lot better shape."

"You said Grabow killed her."

"I know."

"But if Grabow killed her, who killed Grabow?"

"Grabow didn't kill her."

"But it worked out so perfectly. The counterfeiting and the dental scalpels and everything."

"I know."

"So if Grabow *didn't* kill her—"

"Somebody else did. And killed Grabow so that I'd get blamed for it, although why I'd kill that gorilla in my own apartment is something else again. And whoever it was scattered some of Crystal's jewelry around so that I'd be locked into her murder, as if I wasn't already. That would be really intelligent of me, wouldn't it? Killing Grabow with another convenient dental scalpel and then tucking one of Crystal's bracelets under the corpse."

"Is that where they found it?"

"How in hell do I know where they found it? Nyswander

found it, whatever the hell it was. Diamonds, emeralds, I don't know. I haven't seen any of that garbage since I got it all packed up for someone else to steal. How the hell do I know where it was? I barely remember what it looked like."

"You don't have to snap at me, Bernie."

"I'm sorry," I said. "I've got my head in a frame and I can't think straight. It's all crazy, it's all circumstantial evidence and it doesn't make any sense, but I think they've got enough to nail me."

"But you didn't do it," she said, and then her gaze narrowed slightly. "You *said* you didn't do it," she said.

"I didn't. But if you put twelve jurors in a box and showed them all this evidence and I stood up there and said I didn't do it and they should believe me because it would have been stupid for me to do it that way—well, I know what my lawyer would say. He'd tell me to make a deal."

"What do you mean?"

"He'd arrange for me to plead guilty to a reduced charge. And the District Attorney's office would be glad to get a sure conviction without the hazard of a trial, and I'd cop a plea to something like manslaughter or felony murder and I'd wind up with, I don't know, five-to-ten upstate. I could probably be back on the street in three years." I frowned. "Of course it may be different with Grabow dead, too. With two corpses in the picture they'd probably hold out for Murder Two and even with good behavior time and everything I'd be out of circulation for upward of five years."

"But if you were innocent, how could your lawyer make you plead guilty?"

"He couldn't make me do anything. He could advise me."

"That's why Craig switched lawyers. That man Blankenship just assumed he was guilty, and Mr. Verrill knew he wasn't."

"And now Craig's out on the street."

"Uh-huh."

"Even if I had a lawyer who believed in me, he'd have to be crazy to go to court with what they've got against me."

She started to say something but I wasn't listening. I felt a thought slipping around somewhere in the back of my mind and I went after it like a dog trying to catch his tail.

I got the phone book. What was Frankie's last name? Ackerman, Frances Ackerman. Right. I found her listed as *Ackerman F* on East Twenty-seventh Street, just a few blocks from all her favorite bars. I dialed the number and listened to the telephone ring.

"Who are you calling, Bernie?"

I hung up, looked up Knobby Corcoran's number, dialed it. No answer.

I tried Frankie a second time. Nothing.

"Bernie?"

"I'm in a jam," I said.

"I know."

"I think I'm going to have to turn myself in."

"But if you're innocent—"

"I'm wanted on murder charges, Jillian. Maybe I'll even wind up copping a plea. I hate the idea, but it looks as though I might not have any choice. Maybe I can get lucky and some new evidence will come to light while I'm awaiting trial. Maybe I can hire a private detective to investigate this thing professionally. I'm not having much luck as an amateur. But if I keep running around like this I'm taking the chance of getting shot by some trigger-happy cop. And the corpses are just piling up around me and I'm scared. If I'd turned myself in a day ago nobody could have framed me for Grabow's murder."

"What are you going to do? Go down to police headquarters?"

I shook my head. "Kirschmann wanted me to surrender to him. He said I'd be safe that way. All he wanted was to be credited with the pinch. What I want is to have a lawyer present when I turn myself in. They can keep you incommunicado for seventy-two hours, just shuttling you around from one precinct to another without formally booking you. I don't know that they'd do that to me but I don't want to take any chances."

"So do you want to call your lawyer?"

"I was just thinking about that. My lawyer's always been fine at representing me because I've always been guilty as charged. But what good would he be at representing an innocent man? It's exactly the same problem Craig had with Errol Blankenship."

"So what do you want to do?"

"I want you to do me a favor," I said. "I want you to call Craig. I want him to get hold of his lawyer, What's-his-name, Verrill, and I want the two of them to meet me in his office."

"Mr. Verrill's office?"

"Let's make it Craig's office. That way we all know where it is. Central Park South, nice convenient location. It's twelve-thirty now so let's set the meeting for four o'clock because I've got a couple of things I have to do first."

"You want Craig there too?"

I nodded. "Definitely, and if he doesn't show up tell him I'm going to throw him to the wolves. He set me on the hunt for Crystal's jewelry. That fact is the only trump card I've got. The last thing he wants is for me to tell the police about our little arrangement, and there's a price for my silence. I want Verrill on my side. I want him to arrange the surrender to the police and I want the best defense money can buy. Maybe Verrill will wind up hiring a criminal lawyer to assist, maybe he'll bring in private eyes. I don't know how he'll do it and we can arrange that this afternoon, but if the two of them don't show up on schedule you can tell Craig I'll sing my little heart out."

"Four o'clock at his office?"

"That's right." I reached for my jacket. "I've got some things to do," I said. "Some places to go. Make sure they get there on time, Jillian." I went to the door, turned toward her. "You come along, too," I said. "It might get interesting."

"Are you serious, Bernie?"

I nodded. "I'm a threat to Craig," I told her. "If that's my trump card, I don't want to throw it away. He and Verrill might agree to anything just to get me to turn myself in. Then they could forget all about it and leave me stranded after I told my story the way I promised. I want you around as a witness."

I had a busy afternoon. I made some phone calls, I took some cabs, I talked to some people. All the while I kept looking over my shoulder for cops, and now and then I saw one. The city's overflowing with them, on foot and in cars, uniformed and otherwise. Fortunately none of the ones I saw were looking for me—or if they were I saw them first.

A few minutes after three I found the man I was looking for. He was in a Third Avenue saloon. He had his elbow on the bar and his foot on the brass rail, and when he saw me coming through the front door his eyes widened in recognition and his mouth curved in a smile.

"Cutty on the rocks," he said. "Get your ass over here and have a drink."

"How's it going, Dennis?"

"It's going. That's all you can say for it. How's it with you, Ken?"

I extended my hand horizontally, palm down, and wagged it like an airplane tipping its wings. "So-so," I said.

"Ain't it the truth. Hey, Ace, bring Ken here a drink. Cutty on the rocks, right?"

Ace was wearing a sleeveless undershirt and an uncertain expression. He looked like a sailor who'd given up trying to find his way back to his ship and was making the best of a bad situation. He made me a drink and freshened Dennis's and went back to the television set. Dennis picked up his glass and said, "You're a friend of Frankie's, right? Well, here's to Frankie, God love her."

I took a sip. "That's a coincidence," I said, "because I was trying to get hold of Frankie, Dennis."

"You don't know?"

"Know what?"

He frowned. "I saw you last night, didn't I? 'Course I did, you were drinking coffee. We were talking with Knobby. And I was waiting for Frankie to show up."

"That's right."

"She never showed. You didn't hear, Ken? I guess you didn't. She took her own life, Ken. Booze and pills. There was something bothering her about her friend, girl named Crystal. You know about Crystal, don't you?" I nodded. "Well, she had some drinks and she took some Valium. Who's to say if she did it on purpose or if it was an accident, right? Who's to say?"

"Not us."

"That's the truth. A hell of a nice woman and she took her life, accidentally or on purpose and who's to say, and God rest her is all *I* got to say."

We drank to that. I'd been looking for Frankie, at her place, at some of the bars in the neighborhood. I hadn't heard what happened to her but the news didn't surprise me. Maybe it was an accident. Maybe it was suicide. Or maybe it was neither and maybe she'd had help, the kind of help Crystal Sheldrake and Walter Grabow had had.

He said, "I had a whatchacallit last night. A premonition. I sat there all night with Knobby, coasting on the drinks and trying her number from time to time. I was there waiting for her till Knobby closed the joint. Maybe I could of gone over there, done something."

"When did Knobby close up, Dennis?"

"Who knows? Two, three o'clock. Who pays attention? Why?"

"He went back to his place but he didn't stay there. He packed a suitcase and left right away."

"Yeah? So?"

"Maybe he got on a plane," I said. "Or maybe he met somebody and got into trouble."

"I don't follow you, Ken. What's Knobby got to do with what happened to Frankie?"

I said, "Well, I'll tell you, Dennis. It's sort of complicated."

Twenty

I was ten minutes early at the Central Park South office. I'd spoken to Jillian around two-thirty and she'd told me that the meeting with Craig and his lawyer was all set, but I wasn't surprised that they weren't there when I arrived and I had the feeling they wouldn't show at all. I planted myself in the hallway beside the frosted glass door, and at 3:58 on my watch the elevator doors opened and all three of them emerged, Craig and Jillian and a tall slender man in a vested black pinstripe suit. When he turned out to be Carson Verrill I was not wildly astonished.

Craig introduced us. The lawyer shook my hand harder than he had to and showed me a lot of his teeth. They were good teeth, but that didn't surprise me either, because it stood to reason that he patronized the World's Greatest Dentist. We stood there, Verrill and I shaking hands and Craig shifting his weight from foot to foot and clearing his throat a lot, while Jillian sifted through her purse until she found the key and unlocked the office door. She switched on the overhead light and a lamp on Marion the Receptionist's desk. Then she sat in Marion's chair and I motioned Craig and Verrill to the couch before turning to shut the outer door.

There was a little nervous chatter, Craig supplying something about the weather, Verrill saying he hoped I hadn't been waiting long. Just a few minutes, I said.

Then Verrill said, "Well, perhaps we should come to the point, Mr. Rhodenbarr. It's my understanding that you have something to trade. You've threatened to tell the police some story of my client's alleged involvement in a burglary of his ex-wife's apartment unless he underwrites the cost of your defense."

"That's really something," I said.

"I beg your pardon?"

"To be able to talk like that right off the bat. It's an amazing talent, but can't we put our cards on the table? Craig arranged for me to knock off Crystal's place. We're all friends here and we all know that, so what's with this alleged business?"

Craig said, "Bernie, let's do this Carson's way, huh?"

Verrill glanced at Craig. I got the impression that he didn't appreciate Craig's support quite so much as he'd have appreciated silence. He said, "I'm not prepared to acknowledge anything of the sort, Mr. Rhodenbarr. But I do want to get a firm understanding of your position. I've talked with Miss Paar and I've talked with Dr. Sheldrake and I think I may be able to help you. I don't have a criminal practice and I don't see how I could undertake to prepare a defense per se, but if your interest lies in turning yourself in and arranging a guity plea—"

"But I'm innocent, Mr. Verrill."

"It was my understanding—"

I smiled, showing some good teeth of my own. I said, "I've been framed for a pair of murders, Mr. Verrill. A very clever killer has been setting me up. He's not only clever. He's adaptable. He originally arranged things so that your client would wind up framed for murder. Then he found it would be more effective to shift the frame onto my shoulders. He's done a pretty good job, but I think you'll be able to see a way out for me if I explain what I think actually happened."

"Miss Paar says you suspected this artist of murder. Then he was in turn murdered in your apartment."

I nodded. "I should have known he didn't kill Crystal. He might have strangled her or beaten her to death but stabbing wasn't Grabow's style. No, there was a third man, and he's the one who did both killings."

"A third man?"

"There were three men in Crystal's life. Grabow, the artist.

Knobby Corcoran, a bartender at a saloon in the neighborhood. And the Legal Beagle."

"Who?"

"A colleague of yours. A lawyer named John who occasionally made the rounds of the neighborhood bars with Crystal. That's all anybody seems to know about him."

"Then perhaps we ought to forget about him."

"I don't think so. I think he killed her."

"Oh?" Verrill's eyebrows climbed up his high forehead. "Then perhaps it would help if we knew who he was."

"It would," I agreed, "but it's going to be hard to find out. A woman named Frankie told me that he existed. She'd say 'Heeeeeeeeere's Johnny!' just the way Ed MacMahon does it. But sometime last night she drank a lot of gin and swallowed a whole bottle of Valium and died."

Craig said, "Then how are you going to find out who this Johnny is, Bernie?"

"It's a problem."

"Maybe he doesn't even fit in. Maybe he was just another friend of Crystal's. She had a lot of friends."

"And at least one enemy," I said. "But what you have to remember is that she was at the hub of something and somebody had to have a good reason to kill her. *You* had a reason, Craig, but you didn't kill her. You were framed."

"Right."

"And I had a reason—to avoid getting arrested for burglary. I didn't kill her either. But this Johnny had a real reason."

"And what was that, Bern?"

"Grabow was a counterfeiter," I explained. "He started out as an artist, turned himself into a printmaker, and then decided to forget the artsy-fartsy stuff and go for the money. With his talents, he evidently figured that the easiest way to make money was to make money, and that's what he did.

"He was good at it. I saw samples of his work and they were just about as good as the stuff the government turns out. I also saw the place where he lived and worked, and for an unsuccessful artist he lived damn well. I can't prove it, but I've got a hunch he made those counterfeit plates a couple of years ago and passed bills himself, moving them one at a time across bars and cigarette counters. Remember, the man was an artist, not a professional criminal. He didn't have mob connections and didn't know anything about wholesaling big batches of schlock bills. He just ran off a few at a time on his hand-cranked printing press, then passed them one by one. When he had enough turned into real money he went and got himself some good furniture. It was a one-man cottage industry, and he could have gone on with it forever if he didn't get too greedy."

"What does this have to do with—"

"With all of us? You'll see. I'd bet that Grabow covered a lot of ground, stopping in a bar long enough to cash a twenty, then moving on to another one. Somewhere along the way he ran into Crystal and they started keeping company. And maybe he wanted to show off or maybe she asked the right questions, but one way or another she learned he was a counterfeiter.

"She was already having a now-and-then affair with Knobby Corcoran. He was a bartender, but he was also a pretty savvy guy who probably knew how things could be bought and sold. Maybe it was her idea, maybe it was Knobby's, but I'd guess that the lawyer was the one who came up with it."

"Came up with what?" Jillian wondered.

"The package. Grabow was printing the stuff up and unloading it a bill at a time. But why should he do that when he could wholesale a big batch of the stuff and coast on the proceeds for a year or two? The stuff he was turning out would change hands at a minimum of twenty cents on the dollar in large lots. If he could set up a deal for a quarter of a million dollars' worth, he could put fifty thousand dollars in his pocket and not wear out his liver buying drinks in bars all over town.

"So the lawyer set it up. He had Crystal show Knobby some sample twenties. Then Knobby could find somebody who was willing to pay fifty thou, say, for the counterfeit. Crystal would be in the middle. She'd get the real dough from Knobby and the schlock from Grabow, and she'd turn the dough over to Grabow and pass on the counterfeit to Knobby, and that way they wouldn't ever have to see each other. Grabow was crazy about his privacy. He didn't want anybody to know where he lived, so he'd be glad to work a deal that kept him out of the limelight."

"And the lawyer set this up, Bern? This guy John?"

I nodded at Craig. "Right."

"What was in it for him?"

"Everything."

"What do you mean?"

"Everything," I said. "Fifty thousand in cash, because he didn't intend for it to go to Grabow. And a quarter of a mill in counterfeit, because that wouldn't go to Knobby. He got each of them to deliver first. They were both sleeping with Crystal so each of them figured he could trust her. Maybe Crystal knew the lawyer was setting up a double cross. Maybe not. But when she got the money from Knobby she turned it over to the lawyer, and then Grabow delivered the counterfeit dough and she told him he'd get paid in a day or two, and then all the lawyer had to do was kill her and he was home free."

"How do you figure that, Mr. Rhodenbarr?"

"He already had the money from Knobby Corcoran, Mr. Verrill. Now he kills Crystal and takes the counterfeit and that's the end of it. He'd have kept his own name out of it. As far as the others are concerned, Crystal's in the middle, setting up the exchange. When she's dead, what are they going to do? If anything, each one figures the other for a double cross. Maybe they kill each other. That's fine as far as the lawyer's concerned. He's home free. He's got the cash in hand and he can look around to make a deal on his own for the counterfeit. If he gets an average price that's another fifty thousand, so the whole deal's worth somewhere around a hundred thousand dollars to him, and there are people in this world who think that's enough to kill for. Even lawyers."

Verrill smiled gently. "There are members of the profession," he said, "who aren't as ethical as they might be."

"Don't apologize," I said. "Nobody's perfect. You'll even run across an immoral burglar if you look long and hard enough." I walked over to the window and looked down at the park and the horse-drawn hansom cabs queued up on Fifty-ninth Street. The sun was blocked by clouds now. It had been ducking in and out of them all afternoon. I said, "Thursday's the night I went to Crystal's apartment looking for jewels. I wound up locked in the closet while she rolled around in the sack with a friend. Then the friend left. While I was picking my way out of the closet Crystal

151

was taking a shower. The doorbell interrupted her. She answered it and the lawyer came on in and stuck a dental scalpel in her heart.

"Then he walked past her to the bedroom. He hadn't just come to kill her. He was picking up the counterfeit money that she was holding, presumably for Knobby. She'd told him Grabow had delivered it previously in an attaché case, and he walked into the bedroom and saw an attaché case standing against the wall.

"Of course it was the wrong case. The case with the counterfeit was probably right there in the closet with me all along. I think that's probably where Crystal had stowed it, because why else would she automatically turn the key and lock me in the closet? She kept her jewelry where it was easy to get at. But there must have been something in that closet that she wasn't used to having around or she wouldn't have been such a fanatic on the subject of keeping the door locked.

"Well, the lawyer just grabbed that attaché case and took off. When he got home and opened it he found a ton of jewelry all rolled up in enough linen to keep it from rattling around. It wasn't what he'd wanted and it was too hot for him to unload it easily, but at least he had the fifty grand in cash free and clear and he could probably raise close to that much again on the jewelry when it was safe to show it around.

"Maybe he even planned to go back and take another shot at the counterfeit money. But Knobby Corcoran didn't give him the chance. Knobby switched shifts with the other bartender the day after Crystal was murdered, and he was the one who broke the police seals on her door and gave her apartment a second run-through. Maybe he knew where to look, maybe she'd said something like 'Don't worry, it's all here on a shelf in my closet.' Because he broke in and went home with the counterfeit money and tucked it away on the shelf in *his* closet."

"How do you know that, Mr. Rhodenbarr?"

"Simple. That's where I found it."

"That's where you—"

"Found the case full of counterfeit twenties. How else would I know about them? I left them there to keep from rattling Knobby."

Jillian knew better. I'd told her something about stowing the funny twenties in the bus locker and hoped she wouldn't pick this time to remember what I'd said. But she had something else on her mind.

"The scalpel," she said. "The lawyer killed Crystal with one of our dental scalpels."

"Right."

"Then he must have been a patient."

"A lawyer named John," Craig said. "What lawyers do we have as patients?" He frowned and scratched his head. "There's lots of lawyers," he said, "and John's not the scarcest name in the world, but—"

"It wouldn't have to be a patient," I said. "Try it this way. Crystal's been to Grabow's loft on King Street. She saw the dental instruments he used for his printmaking work and recognized them as the same line Craig stocks. That was a coincidence and she happened to mention it to the lawyer. And that made his choice of a murder weapon the simplest thing in the world. He'd use one of the dental implements. It would point to Craig, and if Craig somehow managed to get out from under, he could always find a way to steer the cops toward Grabow."

I'd been pacing around. Now I went over and sat on the edge of Marion the Receptionist's desk. "His plan was a pretty good one," I said. "There was just one thing to screw it up and that was me."

"You, Bern?"

"Right," I told Craig. "Me. The cops had you in a cell and you were looking for a way out, and you decided to throw them your old buddy Bernie."

"Bern, what choice did I have?" I looked at him. "Besides," he said, "I knew *I* hadn't killed Crystal, and if you were in her apartment, and one of my scalpels, hell, it started looking as though you were trying to frame *me,* and—"

"Forget it," I said. "You were looking for a way out and you took it. And Knobby broke into the apartment and snatched the counterfeit money, and that break-in made it obvious there was more going on than a simple case of a man killing his ex-wife. The lawyer saw that he had to move quickly. There were loose threads around and he had to tie them off, because if the police ever really checked into Crystal's background his role in the whole affair might start to become evident.

"And he was worried about Grabow. Maybe the two of them had met. Maybe Grabow knew about the lawyer's relationship with Crystal, or maybe the lawyer didn't know for certain just how much talking Crystal might have done. For one reason or another, Grabow was a threat. And Grabow himself was nervous when I saw him. Maybe he got in touch with the lawyer. Anyway, he had to go, and the lawyer decided he might as well kill Grabow and tighten the frame around me at the same time. He managed somehow to get the artist over to my apartment, killed him with another of those goddamned dental scalpels, and planted a couple of pieces of Crystal's jewelry there to tie it all together for the police. Now why I would kill Grabow in the first place, and why I would kill him with a dental scalpel in my own apartment, and why I would then leave Crystal's jewels around, that was all beside the point. It might not make any absolute sense but it would certainly make the police put out a pick-up order on me, and of course that's what they did." I drew a breath, looked at each of them in turn, Jillian and Craig and Carson Verrill. "And that's where we are," I said, "and that's why we're here."

The silence built up rather nicely. Finally Verrill broke it. He cleared his throat. "You see the problem," he said. "You've developed a convincing case against this nameless attorney. But you don't know who he is and I gather it's not going to be terribly easy to track him down. You mentioned a woman, a friend of Crystal Sheldrake's?"

"Frankie Ackerman."

"But did you say she killed herself?"

"She died mixing alcohol and Valium. It could have been an accident or it could have been suicide. She'd been brooding about Crystal and something was on her mind. It's not impossible that she got in touch with the lawyer directly. Maybe he fed her the booze and pills as part of his process of tying off loose ends."

"That sounds a little farfetched, doesn't it?"

"A little," I admitted. "But either way she's dead."

"Exactly. And a chance to identify this lawyer seems to have died with her. Now this bartender. Corcoran? Is that his name?"

"Knobby Corcoran."

"And he has the counterfeit money?"

"He had it the last I saw of it, but that was yesterday evening.

I'd guess he still has it and I'd guess he and the money are a long ways from here. After he closed the bar last night he went home and grabbed a suitcase and left town. I don't think he'll be back. Either all the killings scared him or he'd been planning all along to cross his mob associates. He was living on tips and leavings and maybe the sight of all that money was too much for him. Remember, it looked like a quarter of a million bucks, even if you could only get twenty cents on the dollar for it. I'll bet Knobby took a cab to Kennedy and a plane to someplace warm, and I wouldn't be surprised if a lot of counterfeit twenties turn up in the West Indies between now and next spring."

Verrill nodded, frowning. "Then you don't really have anything to work with," he said slowly. "You don't have any leads to the identity of this lawyer and you don't know who he is."

"Well, that's not exactly true."

"Oh?"

"I know who he is."

"Really?"

"And I've even got some proof."

"Indeed."

I got up from the desk, opened the frosted glass door, motioned Dennis inside. "This is Dennis," I announced. "He knew Crystal pretty well and he was a good friend of Frankie Ackerman."

"She was a hell of a fine woman," Dennis said.

"Dennis, that's Jillian Paar. And this is Dr. Craig Sheldrake, and Mr. Carson Verrill."

"A pleasure," he said to Jillian. "Pleasure, Doc," he said to Craig. And he smiled at Verrill.

To me—to all of us—he said, "That's him."

"Huh?"

"That's him," he said again, pointing now at Carson Verrill. "That's Crystal's boyfriend. That's the Legal Beagle. That's Johnny, all right."

Verrill broke the silence. It took him a while to do it, and first he got up from the chair and extended himself to his full height, and when he spoke the words were on the anticlimactic side.

"This is ridiculous," he said.

What I said wasn't much better. "Murder," I said, "is always ridiculous." I'm not proud of it but that's what I said.

"Ridiculous, Rhodenbarr. Who is this oaf and where did you find him?"

"His name's Dennis. He runs a parking garage."

"I don't just run it. I happen to own it."

"He happens to own it," I said.

"I think he's been drinking. And I think you've taken leave of your senses, Rhodenbarr. First you try to manipulate me into defending you and now you accuse me of murder."

"It does seem inconsistent," I allowed. "I guess I don't want you defending me after all. But I won't need anybody to defend me. You just have to confess to the two murders and the police'll probably drop their charges against me."

"You must be out of your mind."

"I should be, with the kind of week I've had. But I'm not."

"Out of your mind. In the first place, my name's not John. Or hasn't that occurred to you?"

"It was a problem," I admitted. "When I first expected you I wondered if maybe your name was John Carson Verrill and you dropped the John. No such luck. Carson's your first name, all right, and your middle name is Woolford. Carson Woolford Verrill, the man with three last names. But you're the man Frankie Ackerman was talking about. It's pretty obvious, when you stop to think about it."

"I don't follow you, Bernie." Jillian did look puzzled, all right. "If his name is Carson—"

I said, " 'And now, heeeeeeeere's Johnny.' Johnny *Who*, Jillian?"

"Oh!"

"Right. There's millions of people named John, it's hardly a rare enough name to make Frankie go into Ed MacMahon's routine every time she met somebody with the name. But Carson, that's something else again. That's not so common as a first name, and maybe it struck Frankie funny."

"Ridiculous," Verrill said. "I'm a respectable married man. I love my wife and I've always been faithful to her. I was never involved with Crystal."

"You're not that respectable," Jillian said. "You flirt."

"Nonsense."

"You'd have made a pass at me last night. You were sort of moving in that direction. But I wasn't interested and you backed off."

"That's absurd."

"You knew Crystal years ago," I said. "You knew her when she was married to Craig. That's right, isn't it?"

Craig confirmed that it was. "Carson represented me in my divorce," he said. "Hey, maybe that's why I got such a reaming in the alimony. Maybe my trusted attorney was already hopping in the sack with my wife and the two of them teamed up to put me through the wringer." The World's Greatest Dentist let that thought sink in, and his face took on a new set. Murder was one thing, he seemed to be thinking, but shafting a pal in the alimony department was really rotten. "You sonofabitch," he said.

"Craig, you can't believe—"

"I wish I had you in the chair right now. I'd grind your teeth clear to the gum line."

"Craig—"

"You'll have free dental care for the next few years, Mr. Verrill," I said. "Those penitentiary dentists are terrific. You're in for a treat."

He turned on me, and if those weren't a killer's eyes then seeing's not believing. "You're out of your mind," he said. "You have a lot of theories and nothing else. You don't have any proof."

"That's what the bad guy always says in the movies," I said. "That's when you know he's really guilty, when he starts talking about the lack of proof."

"You've got the prattling of a convicted burglar and a drunken car parker. That's all you've got."

"What's this car-parker crap? I don't park the cars. I own the garage."

"But as for hard evidence—"

"Well, it's a funny thing about evidence," I said. "You usually find it when you know what to look for. When the police start showing your photo around it's going to turn out that more people saw you with Crystal than you ever realized. You found a way to get past my doorman last night, and that couldn't have been the hardest thing in the world, but he or someone else in the building will probably remember you. And then there's the jewelry. You didn't plant all of Crystal's stuff at my place because you're too damned greedy for that. Where's the rest of it? Your apartment? A safe-deposit box?"

"They won't find any jewelry."

"You sound pretty confident. I guess you found a safe place for it."

"I never took any jewelry. I don't know what you're talking about."

"Well, there's the counterfeit money. That ought to be enough to hang you."

"What counterfeit money?"

"The twenties."

"Ah, the elusive twenties." He arched an eyebrow at me. "I thought we were to understand that the equally elusive Knobby headed south with them."

"That's what he must have done. But I've got a hunch there was a sample batch that Grabow ran off in advance, because I've got the damnedest feeling there's a couple thousand dollars worth of those phony bills in your office."

"In my office?"

"On Vesey Street. It's funny how deserted the downtown section is on a Sunday. It's as if a neutron bomb got rid of all the people and just left the buildings standing there. I've got a strong hunch there's a thick stack of twenties in the center drawer of your desk, and I'll bet they're a perfect match to the plates in Walter Grabow's loft."

He took a step toward me, then drew back. "My office," he said.

"Uh-huh. Nice place you've got there, incidentally. No view of the park like Craig has, of course, but you can see a little of the harbor from the one window, and that's something."

"You planted counterfeit money there?"

"Don't be silly. Knobby took the money south. How could I plant it?"

"I should have killed you, Rhodenbarr. If I'd known you were in the closet I could have set it all up right then and there. I'd have left it looking as though you and Crystal killed each other. You stabbed her and she shot you, something like that. I could have worked it out."

"And then you could have taken the twenties from the closet while you were at it. It would have simplified things, all right." He wasn't even listening to me. "I had to get rid of Grabow. I'd met him. And she might have talked to him. Knobby was just someone who took her home now and then after a hard night's drinking, but she had a real relationship with Grabow. He could have known my name, could have guessed I was involved."

"So you got him to meet you at my apartment?"

"He thought he was meeting you. I had his phone number. It was unlisted but of course he'd given it to Crystal. I called him, told him to come up to your apartment. I told him I had his counterfeit bills and I'd give them back to him. It wasn't hard getting past your doorman."

"It never is. How did you get into the apartment itself?"

"I kicked the door in. The way they do on television."

So much for my pick-proof locks. One of these days I'll get one of those Fox police numbers like Grabow had. Not that it had done Grabow much good—

"Then when Grabow got there the doorman buzzed upstairs and I told him to send the man up. Naturally the doorman assumed I was you."

"Naturally."

"Grabow said I didn't seem like a burglar. But he wasn't at all suspicious." He considered for a moment. "He was easier to kill than Crystal. He was big and strong, but it wasn't hard to kill him."

"They say it gets easier as you go along."

"I was hoping you'd come. I'd make it look as though you fought and killed each other. But you didn't come home."

"No," I said. I started to say I was at Jillian's, then remembered Craig was there. "I was afraid the police would have the place staked out," I said, "so I got a hotel room."

"I didn't wait that long anyway. I was uncomfortable staying there with his body in the middle of the room."

"I can understand that."

"So I left. The doorman didn't notice me coming or going. And I didn't leave any fingerprints there. I don't think it means that much, a little counterfeit money planted in my desk. I'm a respected attorney. When it comes down to my word against yours, who do you think the police will believe?"

"What about these people, Verrill?"

"What, this drunk from the garage?"

"I own the damn place," Dennis said. "It's not like it was a hot-dog wagon. You talk about a parking garage and you're talking about a piece of profitable real estate."

"I don't think Craig will want to tell the police everything that's come to light," Verrill went on. "And I trust Miss Paar knows which side of her bread holds the butter."

"It won't work, Verrill."

"Of course it will."

"It won't." I raised my voice. "Ray, that's enough, isn't it? Come on out and arrest this son of a bitch so we can all go home."

The door to the inner office opened and Ray Kirschmann came through it. "This is Ray Kirschmann," I told them. "He's a policeman. I let Ray in earlier before I went to pick up Dennis. I suppose that was forward of me, Craig, picking your lock and everything, but it's sort of a habit of mine. Ray, this is Craig Sheldrake. Jillian you've met. This is Carson Verrill, he's the murderer, and this fellow here is Dennis. Dennis, I don't believe I know your last name."

"It's Hegarty, but don't apologize, for God's sake. Here I had your name all wrong myself. I was calling you Ken."

"Mistakes happen."

"Jesus," Ray said to me. "You're the coolest thing since dry ice."

"I've got the guts of a burglar."

"You said it, fella."

"No, as a matter of fact *you* said it. Do you want to read Carson here his rights?"

"The guts of a burglar."

I let him go on thinking so, but weren't we all pretty cool? Dennis was positively gelid, identifying Verrill so beautifully when he'd never seen the man before in his life. If I hadn't introduced him all around, he might just as easily have picked Craig as the elusive Legal Beagle.

And I'm not so sure I had the ice-cold nerves he'd credited me with, either. I have to admit I got pretty shaky when Verrill drew yet another dental scalpel from his jacket pocket while Ray droned on about his right to remain silent. Ray was reading from the Miranda card and didn't even see what was going on, and my jaw dropped and I froze, and then Carson Verrill gave out with a desperate little yelp and stuck the scalpel straight in his own heart. Then I went back to being cool again.

Twenty-One

"The usual thing," I told Jillian. "He spent more than he earned, he dropped some money in the stock market, he got himself in debt up to his ears, and then he misappropriated funds from a couple of estates he was handling. He needed money, and you'd be surprised what people will do for money. He probably started the deal in motion with the idea of picking up a commission of a few grand. Then he saw a way to get the whole thing. Besides, by this time Crystal was probably more of a liability than an asset. The relationship had dragged on for years and here was a way for him to end it once and for all and pick up a hundred thousand dollars in the process."

"He seemed so respectable."

"I guess he didn't kill Frankie Ackerman. He didn't mention it and it's too late to ask him now. I thought she might have called him last night but I guess her death was either an accident or suicide. If he'd killed her he'd have done it with a dental scalpel."

She shuddered. "I was looking right at him when he did it."

"So was I. So was everybody but Ray."

"Every time I close my eyes I see him doing it, stabbing himself in the chest."

It bothered me, too, but I had an image to maintain and wasn't about to show it. "It was considerate of him," I said breezily. "He saved the state the cost of a trial, not to mention the expense of housing and feeding him for a few years. And he gave Craig an opportunity to keep out of the limelight and made Ray Kirschmann a few dollars richer."

And that was neat, wasn't it? A few thousand dollars had changed ownership, moving from Craig to Ray, and as a result certain details of the crime would never find their way into the record books. There hadn't been any burglary, for example. I was never in the place on Gramercy Park. With the right murderer tagged for the murders and nobody in a position to complain, it was easy enough to sweep unpleasant details under the rug.

I leaned back, took a sip of wine. It was nighttime and I was at Jillian's place and I didn't have to worry about the police dropping in. Sooner or later Todras and Nyswander would collect some kind of statement from me, but in the meantime I had other things on my mind.

I moved to put an arm around Jillian.

She drew away.

I stretched, forced a yawn. "Well," I said, "I guess it might not be a bad idea to take a shower, huh? I haven't had a chance to change my clothes, and—"

"Bernie."

"What?"

"I, uh, well, the thing is Craig's coming over soon."

"Oh."

"He said he'd be coming over around nine-thirty."

"I see."

She turned to look at me, her eyes round and sorrowful. "Well, I have to be practical," she said. "Don't I?"

"Sure you do."

"I was upset with him because of the way he acted, Bernie. Well, it's certainly true that some people are better under pressure than others. And different people work well under different kinds of pressure. Craig's a dentist."

"The World's Greatest Dentist."

"When he's doing some tricky work on a patient, he's got nerves of steel. But he wasn't prepared for being arrested and thrown in a jail cell."

"Few people are."

"Anyway, he's serious about me."

"Right."

"And he's a fine man who is well established in a decent profession. He's respectable."

"Carson Verrill was respectable."

"And he's got security, and that's important. Bernie, you're a burglar."

"True."

"You don't save money. You live from one job to the next. You could wind up in jail at any time."

"No argument."

"And you probably wouldn't want to get married anyway."

"Nope," I said, "I wouldn't."

"So I'd be crazy to throw away something solid with Craig for . . . for nothing. Wouldn't I?"

I nodded. "No question about it, Jillian."

Her lower lip trembled. "Then how come I feel *rotten* about it? Bernie—"

It was time to reach out and take her in my arms and kiss her. It was definitely time to do just that, but instead I put my wine glass on the coffee table and got to my feet. "Getting late," I said. "I'm tired, believe it or not. Had a busy day, all that running around and everything. And you want to freshen up so you'll be at your best when Mr. Thirsty drops in. Me, I want to get on home and hang a couple of new locks on my door and take a shower."

"Bernie, we could still, uh, see each other. Couldn't we?"

"No," I said. "No, I don't think we could, Jillian."

"Bernie, am I making a big mistake?"

I gave the question some real thought, and the answer I supplied was the honest one. "No," I said. "You're not."

In the cab heading through the park I had a moment or two where I felt like Sidney Carton. *A far, far better thing that I do, than I have ever done.* And all that crap about how noble it is to lay down one's life for a friend.

Except crap was what it was, all right. Because the World's Greatest Dentist wasn't all that much of a friend, and what was I giving up anyway? She was cute and cuddly and she made good coffee, but lots of women are cute and cuddly and into more interesting things than the polishing of teeth. And I've never met one yet who makes better coffee than I make for myself, with my filter pot and my custom-blended mixture of Colombian and Guatemalan beans.

The closest I came to Sidney Carton was that I was showing a little quiet class, which is about what Carson Verrill did when he died neatly instead of doing something gross like taking a header out the window. Because I could have complicated that young woman's life no end.

I could have told her, for example, who the ardent lover was who'd been with Crystal while I was cooped up in her closet. I could have said it was none other than Craig himself, and the What's-Her-Name he'd said he had to hurry back to was none other than Jillian herself, and I hadn't recognized his voice because the closet muffled it. I don't know if that's true or not. It would explain some of Craig's confused behavior, and I really tried not to hear the voice and might not have recognized it if it was Craig. But I never pursued the question, not then and not later on. To this day I don't know if it was him.

If I'd advanced the theory, though, it certainly could have screwed things up between the two of them.

But why play dog in the manger?

Or I could have told her that burglary wasn't quite the dead-end profession it might appear to be, and that this case, for all the mess it had been, was by no means leaving me destitute. I might have alluded to the quarter of a million dollars worth of queer twenties which, but for a couple thousand planted in Verrill's desk, still reposed in a locker at Port Authority. They hadn't gone anywhere with Knobby, of course, all that double-talk notwithstanding. Knobby'd gotten his ass out of town the minute he saw they were gone, because he knew some mob heavies were going to expect him to turn up with either fifty grand in cash or five times that amount in counterfeit, and since he couldn't do either New York was a lousy place to be.

So I'd find somebody who knew somebody, and if I couldn't get twenty or thirty grand as my end of the transaction, well, I'd be surprised. Of course I could always decide to do it Grabow's way and pass the bills myself one at a time, but for that occupation you don't need the guts of a burglar. You have to have the gall of a con man and the patience of a saint, and that's a hell of a combination.

For that matter, I could have told her Crystal's jewels still existed somewhere, that Verrill couldn't have sold them yet and certainly hadn't stashed them where the police would trip over them. When things cooled down a little I might have a go at turning them up. So there might not be a future in burglary, and God knows there's no pension plan and no retirement benefits, but if there's no future there's a pretty good present with it, and I was coming out with fair compensation for what had been admittedly a pretty rough couple of days.

So I could have had a shot at changing her mind. But if I had to go through all that then she wasn't worth it, so the hell with her.

There's plenty of women in this world.

Like that one I talked to on the phone. Narrowback Gallery. What the hell was her name? Denise. Denise Raphaelson. She'd been lots of fun over the phone, and fun was something Jillian was manifestly not. Cute and cuddly is nice, but after you've done the dirty deed a few times it's nice if you can also lie around and have a few laughs.

Of course she could turn out to be a beast. Or the chemistry in person could be far different from what it had been over the phone. But in a day or three I'd go look at some paintings, and if the signs were right I'd introduce myself, and if it worked that would be nice, and if it didn't that would be okay, too.

Plenty of women in this world.

But where was I going to find another dentist?

About the Author

LAWRENCE BLOCK can pick a lock with a hairpin, but you'll never catch him admitting it. He once served fifteen months in Joliet Prison for removing the little tag from the bottom of his mattress. His other crimes have taken place in books, of which *The Burglar in the Closet* is the nineteenth. His column on fiction appears monthly in *Writer's Digest*. His stories turn up regularly in mystery magazines and frequently wind up in anthologies. He can generally be found in his Greenwich Village apartment, unless he's gone and locked himself out again.